Forlorn Gambit

By Matt Kirkby

Copyright 2011 Matt Kirkby

Chapter One

"Of course the Baronies recognize the significant threat which you face." Hanparn's hard mouthparts clicked together as the Ospma captain spoke the English words with a harsh accent. Most of the words ended with sharp clicks, and Hanparn inhaled at odd times. "The increasing threat to both of our species is unrelenting. Only united can we hope for victory in this war."

"Thank you." Anton Trudeau kept his own voice soft as he attempted to pronounce the alien words clearly.

On the view screen, Hanparn flexed several of his arms in either a full-body twitch, or a gesture of surprise. Each of his twelve arms ended in a cluster of small tentacles—like a Human's fingers.

From the way Hanparn's skin is mottling, I don't think I quite managed to say what I wanted too, Trudeau noted to himself as purple blotches appeared on the Ospma's lilac-coloured skin. Human mouths were simply not capable of making the harsh clicks that formed the basis of the Ospma language. *It's a minor wonder that we can manage to communicate with each other at all. At least in face-to-face meetings.* Computer translation software was a wonderful invention—and absolutely vital to maintain the close ties between the Human and Ospma worlds. *Only some of us can become fluent in understanding each other, but a full mastery of speaking usually eludes even the most talented of us.* A simple, and unfortunate, matter of genetic design. "We both fight against a foe who would destroy us without hesitation."

"Your war-bands will meet the enemy and surprise them with your ferocity."

Trudeau smiled towards the camera, knowing that Hanparn would recognize the facial expression. "I can only hope that we live up to your belief in us."

"You have never failed us, even after centuries of battle." The Ospma could not smile, of course, but it lifted its multiple arm-tentacles and waved them in a complex salute.

Trudeau felt another amused smile twist at his mouth. Even after decades of contact and interaction, there was still something quite bizarre in having a simple conversation with a twelve-armed starfish, let alone watching it perform a salute. "We *have* failed," he reminded the Ospma. "The Devastators have ravaged across known space without our being able to stop them."

"*All* species have failed to stop them."

Trudeau winced at the harshness in Hanparn's voice. *No need for translation software with him. He's quite fluent.* But, Hanparn had been the ranking Ospma fleet commander for several years.

"The war continues in many star systems."

"I am aware of the current deployment of the Spacey's fleet assets."

"Your warriors fight with dedication. No surrender. No abandonment of colonies and worlds to the Devastators."

"The UHW Spacey *will* fight to the bitter end." That was no simple boast. He knew that only by utterly destroying the Devastators could any world hope to survive the endless war.

The Human suppressed a sudden shiver. The temperature onboard the Human-accessible sections of the *Warsphere* were generally kept much cooler than he, personally, would have preferred. The air was quite damp as well. The Ospma home world was an extremely hot and humid world, with most of its landmasses covered in air-breathing coral, and prone to fierce storms.

A world of atolls instead of continents, Trudeau thought. *With more surface water than Earth, and an environment less than friendly to any species other than the Ospma.* A pity that the Ospma had overreacted to Humanity's dislike of the heat and nearly ninety-nine percent humidity that they preferred. *They've dropped the temperatures almost too low.* But it was not something anyone had been able to fix—or cared enough about to bother with. *Just wear a heavier jacket when attending a meeting,* Trudeau reminded himself.

Most of Hanparn's twenty-three eyes clouded over for a moment. He was clenching a thin wire in one of his tentacles, listening to a report from some other section of the ship.

Trudeau appreciated the efforts that his allies had made. *Converting sections of their largest warships into being suitable for Humans could not have been cheap or easy for them.* He had toured *Warspheres* before—and such tours had required scuba gear for most of the chambers. *Between the water and the atmospheric mix, I am not eager to take another such tour.*

Trudeau tried to suppress another shiver as the ventilation system cycled on and a cold breeze washed over him. "The Devastators continue to close in around our worlds."

"The enemy is relentless." The Ospma paused and reached for another control wire with one of his lilac-coloured tentacles. "More comfort is desired?"

"I dressed appropriately for this visit," Trudeau replied as he adjusted the way in which his jacket fit. *At least, I thought I had. The height of current Earth fashion is, of course, lost upon our allies.* "I am comfortable enough." He would make do—the *Warsphere's* life support systems were geared towards Ospma, not Humans. "I had hoped to speak with the Baron during his upcoming visit to the region."

"The press of his duties may not allow that."

"Of course." The leader of the United Human Worlds nodded his head. *But then why would the Baron bother to come to Earth? Why risk traveling through the war-torn systems?*

Anton Trudeau took another breath of the damp air and desperately attempted to prevent a sneeze. There was a definite hint of the sea in the air. *Or is that Hanparn?* It was difficult to be certain.

If the Human smelled, the Ospma gave no notice.

* * *

The fabric of space rippled and shimmered and then a wormhole swirled open like a giant red eye. Bolts of bright lightning crackled around its perimeter while the heart of the tunnel was the black of deepest space.

"Wormhole stable."

"Thank you, Lieutenant Belanger." Brad Chambers stood near the floor-to-ceiling windows of the space station's command deck and smiled as he watched ships emerge from the whirlpool. He stood with his hands clasped behind his back, the image of a commander at ease. He ignored the sudden shuddering of the deck plates beneath his boots.

Small flashes appeared within the wormhole's heart.

"We have ships emerging. All gunners are on alert status."

"Maintain alert, but hold all fire until I order otherwise." Brad nodded his head, though he continued to stare through the viewport. *It* could *be an attack, but it's not very likely.* "Magnify," he ordered and a panel set into the window rippled.

There was no mistaking the blocky hulls of the UHW Spacey fleet.

Chambers could see *Deliverance* cruisers, *Torrential* missile frigates, and a pair of *Endor* scout frigates leading the way. Their formations were followed by globular Ospma *Warspheres* and *Battleglobes.*

I never get tired of seeing that sight, Brad thought to himself. And *Leonidas* Station, guarding the zenith worm-point, had one of the best viewpoints. *Perhaps they opened the wormhole a little closer to the station than per procedure,* he thought, recalling the manner in which the deck plates had shuddered. *No doubt the Ospma want to show off their superior navigation systems.*

"All codes are confirmed. It's the Tenth Battle Squadron."

"Good to see them here." Chambers turned towards his command staff. "Order the gunners to stand down. My compliments to Admiral Sawyer for her timely arrival here."

Lieutenant Alex Milne gestured to one of the displays. "Looks like a fair-sized flotilla of Ospma came along."

"Always good to have company visit." Chambers frowned at the magnified visual display. "What are those big ones?" he asked. *I don't think I've seen those kinds of ships before.* "They look too big to be Scout Wheels."

"Science vessels, I think."

"Get me a closer scan, Belanger."

The sensor officer nodded her head. Her fingers flew across her keyboard, inputting commands as quickly as she could type "I can't get a clean scan on them, Director. There's some interference. I'll try to compensate for it."

"Do your best." Chambers frowned again. *What could be causing the interference?* He walked towards the communications station. "Any transmissions from them, Mister Lynch?"

Jackson Lynch shook his head. "Just standard system arrival notices. Identification transponders, etcetera."

Chambers grimaced. "I do not like surprises."

Three of the huge disk-shaped ships, with a trio of *Battleglobe* escorts, abruptly broke away from the Tenth Battle Squadron, and accelerated away from the regular traffic lanes.

"They're heading in-system."

Chambers turned his head to another officer. "Towards Earth?"

Michelle Belanger shook her head. "Not on that vector, Director." She turned to her console and began manipulating controls. "I'll try to plot their course."

"They headed off with just a few of their escorts," Milne pointed out.

"I noticed that."

The command deck's hatch hissed open and a pomegranate-coloured, ten-armed Ospma slithered through.

"Gorpshan." Chambers offered him a polite nod, though he was not positive that the Ospma would recognize the gesture as such. "The Tenth Battle Squadron has just arrived, with Ospma escorts. They brought some new ships along with them. Big disk-shaped ones. We're not used to seeing that design of Ospma vessels."

Gorpshan slowly crept across the floor in an undulating motion. "Guild of Science requires readings to be taken of your star." His sucking-clicking accent was heavy, but still understandable.

"What kind of readings?" Chambers frowned. "We have our own array of scientific satellites around the sun, and throughout the rest of the solar system for that matter. Quite an extensive one, for that matter. We could have transmitted the readings for you."

"Guild requires precise readings." Mauve patches rippled across the Ospma's leathery skin. "Precision is vital." His tentacles twitched.

"We know all how vital precision is, Gorpshan. We *do* control the wormholes."

"With our guidance."

Chambers nodded, conceding that point. The Ospma had helped extensively with the building of *Leonidas*, and its sister station, *Masada*, at the nadir pole. The Ospma had given wormhole technology to the Humans and allowed them to build dozens of colonies. *And all of their electromagnetic scanning technology is still superior to ours*, he thought with just a touch of bitterness. "Quite an escort you sent along with your science ships," he said.

"Repairs needed. Sol Yards closer than Barony Yards."

"Your forces fought a stern battle against the Devastators then?"

"Many battles. Many foes." Abruptly, Gorpshan undulated towards the hatch. "I go." Given the shape of his body, he didn't even need to bother turning around.

With that body shape, one direction is as good as any other I guess, Chambers noted. The Ospma had a ring of eyes around his body so he never had to turn around. *No sneaking up on him either.*

* * *

"This is going to be the greatest gathering of warships in history."

"We're defending our home world from destruction, Corwin." Admiral Dale Arden kept his tone light even as he pretended that the shuttle ride was a lot smoother than it actually was. "Of course we're going to call back every ship we can. The full mustering of the Seven Fleets will be needed."

Securely strapped into his own chair, David Corwin frowned. "But won't that leave our colonies vulnerable to attack?"

"Yes, our *remaining* colonies will have to fend for themselves at least for a time." Arden paused. "This shift in deployment won't be forever. We'll be able to respond to colonial distress signals in good time should an attack be launched."

"So you hope."

The admiral sighed under his breath. "If the Devastators really have determined the coordinates for Earth, then they will strike at us with overwhelming force. The UHW Spacey has to muster whatever we can if we're going to stop them." His gaze drifted to the windows and the array of orbital weapon platforms that past generations of military minds had erected to defend humanity's birthplace.

Most of the defense grid was composed of standard *Robin Hood*-class *OWPs*, each platform armed with two missile racks and three surge cannons. The missiles would engage enemy warships while the surge cannons would shoot down fighter-drones or enemy missiles.

"Do you have any idea of what those orbital weapon platforms cost, Admiral?" Anton Trudeau had compained during one budget meeting.

"Two hundred and fifty megadollars apiece," Arden had replied without having to consult his datapad. "And the heavy OWPs are seven hundred and fifty."

"We could have built a scout ship or missile frigate for the cost of one of those heavy OWPs."

"Yes, but in many cases the OWPs offer more firepower...no need for maneuverability or crew life support. Just pure firepower."

There were only a handful of the heavy OWPs currently in orbit, but each of them carried double the firepower of their smaller brethren.

"Impressive hardware. They look strong enough to hold off a fleet."

"I just hope we never have to test them." Arden paused as the shuttle lurched slightly. *If the war comes here, then we will have already lost.*

Corwin's green eyes narrowed as the shuttle rocked again. "Our pilot needs some more time in the simulator."

"We were all young once."

"Speak for yourself."

The intercom crackled. *"We should be coming up on Spaceguard-One shortly. Our ETA is twenty minutes."*

"Five hundred years and we still can't build intercoms without static." Arden's lips twitched in a slight smile.

Corwin just looked at him.

"Well, it's true, isn't it?"

"I suppose."

Arden looked back out of the porthole. "The fleet is already gathering," he commented. There were a lot of warships in orbit, alongside the *OWPs* and space stations. *And more ships on the way.*

It *would* be quite a gathering.

* * *

"Incoming drones!"

Collin Zane cursed under his breath as Christoph Wolfgang's warning echoed across the bridge. "Fire counter batteries." *Those damned things are so fast and agile—and UHW Spacey ships generally aren't.* "Kemp, get me a targeting solution on that carrier! Jankowski, evasive maneuvers!"

"Aye, Captain!"

"It's too late!"

The *Hellstorm* rocked as two of the slender drones broke though the frigate's web of defensive fire and collided directly against its hull.

"Hull breached!" Wolfgang called out. "Ventral hull, port side. Damage control teams are responding!"

Zane coughed as acrid smoke puffed through the ventilator system. "Let's hope not too many of them are programmed as kamikazes," he said. *Bad enough taking laser fire from those swarms. Direct collisions would cause a lot more damage.*

"We have a target lock...carrier bearing five seven mark three one."

"Give them a barrage."

"Missiles launched." Gerald Kemp hunched over his board as the *Hellstorm* lurched again. "Bearing on target."

"Jankowski, take us evasive!"

"Aye, Captain."

"Missile impacts! Reading hull damage...their defences are down, Captain."

"Destroy them!"

"Shunting power to forward batteries."

Zane smiled grimly at Gerald Kemp's eager tone. The *Hellstorm* was an old ship, but still serviceable. It was an early generation Earth-built *Witch of Endor*-class scout frigate, later retrofitted with one of the Ospma's artificial quantum singularities and electromagnetic weaponry. "Fire!" he shouted and terrawatts of raw power were shunted to the warship's primary weaponry.

Armour-plating on the egg-shaped carrier shattered as a powerful energy bolt lanced into its hull.

"Didn't expect that, did you?" Zane crowed. The *Hellstorm* looked like a *Witch of Endor* scout frigate, but the secondary sensor array had been destroyed long ago and replaced by an electromagnetic bolter during the necessary repairs.

"Direct hit on target. Reading extensive power fluctuations."

Zane frowned. "But they're not breaking off."

"No, Captain."

"They never do." Zane cursed under his breath. "Give them another missile volley! Quickly, while their defences are down."

"Reading new power signatures!" Wolfgang warned. "Additional waves of drones are now launching."

"I thought we'd destroyed all their drones."

"They must have kept some back. Get us out of here!" Zane ordered.

Jankowski leaned over his console. "The helm is sluggish...we've taken some reactor damage." A microscopic singularity powered the ship, with a mag-gravitic reactor harnessing the energy of the miniature black hole and regulating it to power the engines, sensors, weaponry, and other systems.

"Get out and push if you have too. Kemp, get the weapon batteries operating. I want cover fire."

"Surge cannons are recharging." Kemp sounded unflappable. No matter how grim the odds, no matter how fierce the battle, he was a steady rock. "All gunners are ready to swat drones."

Zane smiled, then he irritably swatted a floating piece of debris away from his face. *Damned inconvenience.* Someday scientists would figure out a way to generate gravity onboard a ship.

"Take us about. Set course for Moria Prime. Wolfgang, open a comm-channel with the colonial governor. Inform him that the evacuation can proceed."

"Aye, Captain."

· **Chapter Two**

"Once, our Parliament consisted of Members representing over fifty colonies scattered across thirty-seven star systems....now I will be addressing a mere *twenty*. The once vast United Human Worlds are now reduced to twenty...and that number continues to dwindle." Anton Trudeau shook his head sadly as he stared through the windows of his tenth floor office out into the building's Green Well. He ignored the carved wood paneling and plush carpeting of his office. Part of him was still out in space, onboard Hanparn's *Warsphere*.

"Don't be so glum, Prime Minister." Trevor Ross offered a friendly smile from where he was sitting on a plush leather-upholstered chair. "Most of those worlds were lost long before you were ever elected as a city mayor."

"That doesn't do much to raise my spirits," Trudeau said sourly.

"The war has been a long and difficult one." Cynthia Randal was dressed in a floor-length dress, in her usual somber colours. Her hair was coiled into an intricate braid.

"And it will continue to be." Trudeau turned back towards his aides. "Too many generations of Humanity's bravest have been sacrificed in this damned war."

"Our Ospma allies are losing colonies as well."

Cynthia nodded her agreement with Trevor's statement. "The war defines us."

Trudeau grimaced. "The war *weakens* us," he told them. "We've wasted trillions of dollars in fighting this war. We've expended uncounted resources which could have been spent helping our colonists building warships and weaponry."

"We have had little choice, Prime Minister."

"And even with the largest military force in history, billions of people have still died. Soldiers and civilians alike."

"The Devastators must be stopped…that particular fact cannot be doubted." Cynthia's tone certainly held no doubt. "Any and all attempts at negotiation have failed completely. The Devastators don't want to talk. They only want to see us destroyed."

Trevor snorted. "They're *machines*…how can they *want* anything?"

Trudeau turned back to the windows. "I am going for a walk. Alone." He stared at his aides for a moment. "Remain here."

"Are you certain?"

"Yes, I am." He paced towards the door. "I just a new bit of time to think."

Cynthia glided across the carpet. "Just remember, you have a press conference at four o'clock." She adjusted his tie, tightening it. "You won't want to be late for that."

"No, the press might actually have to broadcast something without my face attached to it." Trudeau chuckled. "That would be a novelty."

* * *

"Where are those damned drones?"

"Circling around for another pass."

Zane cursed softly. He glanced down at his fingers—he was clenching the arms of his chair so tightly that his knuckles were white. He forced himself to loosen his grip. "Get me a targeting lock."

"Surge cannons are operating at minimal power, Captain. Repairs to the power grid will take some time."

"Minimal power is all we need for this. Do your best, Kemp."

"Tracking now." Gerald Kemp watched the screens closely. The targets were small—the drones were barely six meters in length—and highly maneuverable. "Firing surge cannons!" He relayed the orders to the gunners and he grinned as the batteries opened up. *One hit, one kill,* he thought as multiple bolts struck into the approaching squadron.

The *Hellstorm* shuddered as surviving fighter-drones raked its hull with particle bolts.

"Minimal damage to the hull. No breaches this time."

"Surge cannons are still firing," Kemp announced. "The last of the drones has been destroyed."

Zane exhaled in relief. "That's good news." *We might survive this after all.* He hoped they would. *Moria Prime is relying on us.*

"Captain?" Wolfgang's voice rose. "Enemy command ship on approach vector."

"Damn it!" Swallowing hard, Zane's eyes flicked to the main display. "Just the one?"

"So far."

"One's all that those machines will need," Kemp muttered.

Zane ignored the comment and studied the tactical display. Defending the ring-shaped space station was his primary concern. *The colony has to be guarded...we can't move away or else we'll leave it vulnerable.* He was tied down strategically and tactically. *If we hold our position, then we'll get pounded by the drones from the Devastator.* It was a no-win situation.

Devastator tactics remained fairly consistent—swarm any enemy warship or station with drones until destroyed, and then move into range to sweep up the debris.

We're going to need a lot of firepower to take down that brute. The Devastator command ship was massive and powerful. It dwarfed even the Human-built starbase. "Remember, Devastators *can* be destroyed." Zane tried to sound confident. "We've all seen the visuals from Londinium." *Of course, that* victory *cost the Fourth Fleet almost half its total strength. Over a hundred cruisers and frigates were lost.*

Kemp shook his head. "Captain, the Fourth Fleet was a *fleet*. We're just one ship."

"And the space station and the orbital defences," Zane reminded him.

"Oh, that will make all the difference," Kemp muttered.

Wolfgang gave a start as his console beeped. "New signals...Ospma warships on approach."

"Track them." Zane refused to allow hope to colour his tone. *It's too early to think that we can win this...we're outnumbered. Badly.* "How many are there?" *And where the hell did they come from?* He wasn't aware of any of his allies operating in Moria system.

"One *Warsphere*, five *Battleglobes*, multiple *Resoshexes*, and at least one *Scout Wheel*." Wolfgang frowned. "The *Wheel* must have been masking their presence from us."

"At least the Devastators will be equally surprised." Zane wasn't sure what the Ospma were up too. *They mindset is just a little too* alien *at times.* "Break orbit and move to join their formation. We have to destroy that factory ship."

"Aye, Captain." Jankowski activated the engines.

"Fresh signatures...enemy drones closing fast."

Zane cursed under his breath at Wolfgang's warning. "Any chance of a wormhole?"

"Negative...readings are dead."

"Damn." He was hoping for additional reinforcements to arrive.

"The Ospma are firing!"

A volley of blue energy bolts streaked from the surge cannons of the *Battleglobes*.

Explosions erupted across the dark metallic hull of the *Devastator*. Green bolts of light streaked back from its own batteries.

"The Ospma are fighting well."

"They've had a lot of practice."

Zane cleared his throat. "Contact Moria Prime...they need to accelerate the evacuation."

"Aye, Captain."

"Jankowski, shunt all available power to engines. Take us ahead at full speed. I want a slashing attack—get us in, hit them, and then run."

"Aye, Captain." Jankowski turned back to his console. "Shunting power to engines." One advantage of the Ospma power system was that energy from singularity could be easily rerouted to boast systems like sensors, weaponry, or engine thrust. The deck plates vibrated and the bulkheads groaned as the ship adjusted to the stress.

"Kemp, tie your console into the helm. I want you to hammer that Devastator with everything we've got as we pass."

"Aye, Sir."

"Wolfgang, transmit our course to the Ospma. Maybe we can coordinate our efforts." They had to cripple that command ship or the Moria colony would stand no chance at all.

* * *

Dale Arden's shuttle cut through the last of the cloud layer, and flew over Nanaimo as it decelerated.

The Government Complex was a beautiful work of art. A multileveled wedge-shaped structure, with a truncated point adjacent to a circular park full of statues and fountains.

"It's not raining today."

"For now." Arden kept his tone light. "It was raining earlier." The city looked wet. *It rains almost every day.*

"The landing pad has given us clearance."

"Land then." The rooftop pad was well placed, set back from the open Green Well. *I have no time to pass through the reception lobby on the first floor today.* It would be filled with the usual assortment of politicians and lobbyists and other necessary members of government. "There's no time for any of that nonsense," he muttered.

"What did you say, Admiral?"

"Nothing of importance, Pilot." Arden grimaced. "Just thinking to myself out loud. I must be getting old."

The pilot didn't respond.

Arden turned back towards the porthole.

Arden paced along the marble-tiled corridor in his dark blue uniform. Passing clusters of civilian officials, he felt out of place wearing the full admiral uniform.

It does give me gestures of respect, he thought as minor functionaries hurriedly stepped out of his path. *They must think I'm on a mission.* If any of them actually recognized who he was. *To most of them, I'm probably just another man in uniform.*

There were sentries at the Complex's entrances and a handful who moved through the building on patrols. They recognized him and offered him an appropriate salute.

He returned each greeting, but didn't slow his pace. From the rooftop shuttle pad, he descended to the tenth level where the highest levels of the government had their offices and meeting rooms.

As was his custom, he made himself stop and take a moment to fully appreciate the combination of graceful design and functionality that was the hallmark of the Complex. Many of the arched ceilings, walls, and floors had transparent panels that channeled water from the rain gutters throughout the building. Coloured lights shining through the water added to the ambiance.

"This place is too beautiful to be a place of government."

Arden nodded to the Prime Minister. "I've often thought so myself."

Trudeau was standing in a small alcove containing a statue of one of his predecessors. He was alone.

"I see that you've given your aides the slip for the moment." Arden stroked his moustache. For the umpteenth time, he thought about getting some dye to mask the gray, and just as quickly dismissed the thought as being silly. *With all that's happening, my gray is the last thing I need to worry about. Anyway,* he thought, *I've earned every single strand of gray.*

"They are plotting campaign strategy...I left them to it." Trudeau had loosened his sharp red tie. His black jacket was open as well. *I'm going to be comfortable on this walk,* he thought. *Regardless of what Cynthia thinks it will do to my image.* He gave Admiral Arden a friendly smile. "I was on my way to take a few moments in the Green Well."

"That sounds like a nice way to spend the afternoon," Arden's voice held plain agreement. The Green Well extended from the ground up through the Complex, as if the architect had carved a slice through the building. The ground floor was devoted to an arboretum, and plants hung from balconies up the inner walls to the open ceiling. "I will join you then, if you don't mind my company. I've been in space too long."

"Ah yes, your tour of the Sol System's outer colonies and military bases." The Prime Minister slowly nodded his head. "I trust that you found nothing to complain about."

"There is nothing that needs to be put into a report," Arden replied. "The outer system colonies know their duty every bit as well as the orbital defence network."

"I wondered how Freedom Station would take your visit."

"General Franklin and I have a perfectly cordial relationship."

"That is not what the inter-department gossip hounds would say."

"Some of the officers in the Spacey spend too much time engaged in idle chatter and not enough attending to their duties." Arden tried to sound grim, but then he burst into a chuckle. "If the scientists could just figure out how gossip manages to move faster than light...."

"We could replicate that for normal communications?" Trudeau was also laughing.

"The Green Well should be nice and peaceful. I need to feel some greenery around me."

"Please join me then, Admiral."

"Thank you, Prime Minister."

The two men fell into step together.

The arboretum was peaceful. Mature trees towered over smaller shrubs. Ornate flowerbeds showcased plants from all over Earth.

"Let us wander." Trudeau led the way along one of the moss-covered paths. The moss was a hardy breed, engineered to provide a sidewalk of sorts.

Arden paused to sniff at the blossoms of a sprawling lilac bush.

They walked past one of the dozens of fountains which bubbled contentedly throughout the indoor park.

The trill of birdsong provided a soothing background.

"It's a fine building."

"I have always thought that. Our ancestors did the right thing when they chose to build this place here."

"As opposed to Beijing or Geneva or New York?"

"Quite." Arden looked up towards the sky. *Still sunny*. He could see balconies on the upper floors which opened into the Green Well. "Shouldn't there be more people here?" he asked. They had only passed a dozen or so, at most, during their walk.

"Most of the bureaucrats are still at work, Admiral. We are in-between their lunches so we have a fair amount of privacy." Trudeau offered him a smile. "If you want to see people, then go to the reception hall on the ground floor." He waved offhandedly towards the east. "Or go to the second floor art galleries. The public swarms them."

"I'll pass, thank you." Arden shook his head. They had halted near a fountain. Eight stone fish were spitting water which arched back into a basin. "That would just be *too* many people."

"I know the feeling." Trudeau stooped over so that he could dip his fingers into the cool water. "There are times that the burden of governing the UHW weighs more heavily than I can bear."

"Someone has to carry the burden."

"I know, Admiral, I know."

* * *

"Only forty per cent?" Collin Zane blinked his eyes in dismay. "That's *all*?" he asked.

Director Gordon Bray nodded. He was carefully strapped down into his chair in Zane's cabin. "The evacuation is slow going. We just don't have the transports available to carry everyone."

"You operate a mining colony."

"Yes, I do, Captain."

"You should have lots of transports."

"Ore barges." Bray shook his head grimly. "I have access to numerous *ore* barges, but they're just not designed to transport passengers. I can load the cargo bays with people...but with there's no life support in those holds. Everyone will freeze to death or suffocate long before the barges can reach the worm-point."

Zane grimaced. "And assuming that they can slip past the Devastators in far orbit."

"Indeed. I have techs attempting to modify the air filtration system, but it's slow going."

"Time is *not* an ally of ours. Fleet Command still hasn't responded to my request for reinforcements."

"Nor has Vederman been able to influence Parliament." Bray's mouth twisted. "We've been written off."

"The United Human Worlds doesn't have enough colonies left to write any of them off," Zane argued. "At least we have some Ospma support."

"A *Warsphere* and a handful of *Battleglobes*. Where is the rest of Sixth Fleet?" Bray demanded. "Why are they not here fighting?"

"An excellent question." Zane shrugged and unstrapped himself from his chair. He pushed himself towards a cabinet. He twisted his body around in the zero-gravity environment. "Would you care for a drink, Governor?"

"Good God yes."

Zane removed two bulbs from the cabinet. "I think the name translates into *Dragon's Breath*." He tossed one bulb across the room.

Bray eyed the green liquid with a dubious look as he caught the bulb. "It's safe?" The liquid was slightly luminous.

"Absolutely." Zane sipped through the straw.

Bray broke the seal and squeezed a mouthful of the liquid between his lips. "Shit," he swore after swallowing. "Dragon's *Piss* is more accurate." He grimaced, eying the bulb in distaste. "That's awful!"

"I think the Ospma use it to clean their hulls." Zane grinned as the governor continued his cursing. "I've acquired a taste for it."

"You can have it."

A loud buzz sounded from the intercom.

"*Battle stations!*" a voice called out. "*Devastators on approach vectors.*"

"Damn it." Zane hurried towards the door.

Bray followed, moving slightly slower and more clumsily than the captain. "I'd hoped to get more of the repairs to your ship completed."

"So did I." Zane adjusted his uniform tunic as he swam down the corridor. "This is the captain," he called into his comm-link. "Time to weapons' range?"

"*Five minutes for the first wave of drones,*" Wolfgang replied.

"I'm on my way."

* * *

Trudeau smiled at his wife as he stepped through the door into his home. "It's going to be a quiet evening at home for us tonight, Isabelle. I cleared my calendar...just for you."

She was wearing a low-cut dress, in a shimmering red and green pattern. "Do you like it?"

"Is it new?"

"Just bought it this morning."

"I like it."

"Good." In the privacy of their residence, Isabelle tended to favour clothing styles more suited for a much younger woman. In public, of course, she dressed in a manner more appropriate to the wife of a head of state. "You actually cleared your calendar?"

"I thought you'd like some time alone."

"That is a rarity for you."

Anton smiled sadly. "I feel guilty for leaving you so often."

"I knew the risks when I agreed to marry you," she told him. "You were already a dedicated politician. My parents were colonial leaders, remember, I am perfectly aware that politics comes before marriage."

"It shouldn't! I love you, Isabelle. I should be here more."

"You are here right now...that is enough for me."

"Is it?"

"It will be a treat for us both then." She offered him one of her most seductive smiles. "A real treat."

"A treasure beyond counting," he replied with a broad grin as he took note of just how deeply her neckline plunged. *If the 'nets got a scan of her looking like that, they'd have a field day.*

The comm buzzed.

"Let the machine answer it," Isabelle told him. "We're not home."

"Sounds like the prelude to a good evening then."

"I'll get you a drink."

"And dismiss the servants for the night?"

She looked back over her shoulder. "I already did." She winked.

Still chuckling, the Prime Minister stepped into his small home office and pulled off his tie. His eyes drifted to the south wall where a large painted star map hung. The map showed the extent of the United Human Worlds and its holdings. *Too many of those worlds are lost to us now,* he thought bitterly. *My time in office could mark the final decline of the United Human Worlds and the extinction of the Human race.*

Leaving his tie abandoned on his desk, Trudeau left the room and slammed the door behind him.

Chapter Three

"Warn off the *Ryu-Chi*. Tell them to leave the area."

"Aye, Major."

A second officer pursed his lips as he studied the flickering displays. "They won't run, Major," he said in a grim voice. "Not from this prize."

"I know, Captain Piotrowski."

"*Ryu-Chi* is responding...reminding us that this is still considered neutral space."

"The hell it is." Major Duncan O'Brien shook his head. "We claimed it first."

"Two more vessels moving in," Lieutenant Farnsworth reported from his station. "The computer is scanning their hull markings now."

O'Brien snorted. "More of those damned Japs most likely."

"Idents confirmed...*Hachiman* and *Bishamon*."

"Two known warships."

O'Brien slapped Piotrowski on the shoulder. "Let them come...we've got the firepower to back us up." The space station was heavily armed after all. *We've been shipping in weaponry for nearly two years now. This station has more firepower than a full fleet. More then they will expect it to carry.* "Davids, open an all-channels transmission." He paused a moment until his communications officer finally nodded. "Attention to all ships: LaGrange Three is American territory. The habitats and factories located here are now under our jurisdiction. LaGrange Three is protected by law and I will act to defend our territory with every means at my disposal." He made a chopping gesture across his throat.

"Channel closed."

O'Brien chewed at his lip. "What's their response?"

"Silence on all frequencies, Sir."

"Silence?"

"Yes, Major. They're not transmitting anything right now." Davids paused for a moment. "They're probably using lasers to tight-beam signals."

"Of course they are." O'Brien nodded in agreement. "Comm-lasers can't be tapped into or jammed. They can talk all they want too without us listening in." The officer grimaced. *Total security and privacy for them to make their plans. How the hell do I disrupt those plans?* he wondered. "Location of the enemy fleet?"

Farnsworth did not bother to look up from his console. "All three ships are holding position just beyond optimum weapons range."

"Watch them, Lieutenant. Gun crews, keep the lasers locked onto your chosen targets." O'Brien kept his tone steady. "If they come any closer, burn them out of space."

"Aye, Major."

"They'll back off."

"They always do, Captain." O'Brien nodded. "They always do." He turned his head and raised his voice. "Lieutenant Davids, establish a tight-beam laser link with the *Roosevelt*. I want Captain Goldstein to be prepared to support us."

"Aye, Major."

Without warning, the entire station shuddered.

"What the hell is going on?" O'Brien called out as the bulkheads shook even more violently.

"Some kind of turbulence."

"Turbulence?" O'Brien scoffed. "We're in the middle of open space! There's nothing to cause any bloody kind of turbulence." The bulkheads were groaning as the metal twisted and bent.

"I know, Sir."

"Are we under attack, Davids?" Piotrowski demanded as the deck continued to shift under his feet.

"I'm not sure!"

"Signal Washington!" O'Brien ordered. "This must be some kind of Jap trick."

"Should we order the gunners to open fire?"

O'Brien forced himself to pause and consider Piotrowki's question as he grabbed for the back of a chair to steady himself. The station was no longer rotating smoothly so the artificial gravity was disrupted.

"I'm not sure," he finally admitted. "My impulse is to respond to this attack, but it's not a real attack." The station was not reacting to stabbing laser beams or missile impacts, but it was still shaking. "Order all gunners and ships to stand by."

"Internal radios are down. External radio channels are being jammed."

"Jammed?"

"It's some kind of interference."

"Break through it."

"I'm trying." Davids' fingers typed commands with frantic desperation. "No response...just static on all frequencies."

"Farnsworth, is the fleet under attack?"

"I'm not sure..."

"Regain communications. Use the comm-lasers."

"Tracking arrays are off-line...attempting to compensate."

Piotrowski hurried across the deck to the com-station. "Use the internal lines to contact the gun batteries."

"Major, the shaking!"

"It's stopped."

O'Brien ignored Piotowski's startled exclamation. "Get me a contact with the fleet. Raise the habitats." *If any of them had been destroyed....*

"Still trying to break through the interference."

"Get me a visual!"

"All systems are still stabilizing."

"Then have someone look out a damned window!"

"Major!"

O'Brien turned his head. "What?"

"It's another vessel."

"Whose?"

Farnsworth shrugged. "No idea...it's not like anything I've ever seen before." The image flashed onto a monitor.

O'Brien stared.

The ship was a dark-hulled sphere, bristling with obvious weaponry.

"Is it Japanese?"

"I don't think so."

"Where the hell did it come from?" Major O'Brien demanded. "There's no way in hell it could have snuck up to us!"

Farnsworth shrugged. "It appeared from some kind of disturbance."

"What kind of *disturbance*? I need precise information!"

"I'm not sure, Major." The officer shrugged. "There was a massive energy spike and then a radiation wave washed out the sensors. I'm still trying to clean up what data we did manage to record."

"I see."

"Hopefully one of our other outposts will have picked up something more clear." Piotrowski gestured. "The rest of the habitats appear intact."

"So does our fleet." O'Brien was relieved, even when he saw the trio of Japanese warships still floating beyond laser range. "If it was an attack, it was a poorly aimed one."

"Comm-system is back on-line. The habitats are transmitting...they want to know what just happened."

"No answer. Tell them to clear the air-waves." O'Brien turned his attention to the unknown ship. "I want to know what that thing is."

"It appeared out of some kind of disturbance. Radiation levels are returning to normal. They spiked when that ship appeared."

"So it *is* an attack?"

"I don't think so, Major. We didn't actually take any serious damage from it...I think we just experienced the side-effects of their arrival."

"Some form of faster than light drive?"

"Looked more like a wormhole. I recall seeing a similar effect watching old 'vids."

"So it's alien." O'Brien was startled. *First contact at last.*

"It certainly doesn't look like any ship on record."

"Captain Goldstein is requesting orders."

"Order him to stand by." O'Brien frowned. "First contact with intelligent alien life."

"The stuff that makes history."

"And careers." Then the major grimaced. "Or ends them." O'Brien stared at the monitor. The globe just hung there. "What is it?" *Who could have built that thing?* "Download all of our data to Washington. I want them to know exactly what's happening up here."

"Transmitting on secure frequencies."

"Send a message drone as well." Piotrowski cleared his throat. "We don't want to take any chances with this."

"Good thinking. Send the drone."

The sphere hung in space while O'Brien studied the visual. "No signs of life."

"Could it be a probe?"

"It's awfully big for a probe." Farnsworth swallowed sheepishly as Pitrowski looked at him. "I'd say it's almost the size of this station."

"It's a lot larger than any of the Japs."

"I see that too."

"Major, the unidentified vessel is moving...on approach vector."

O'Brien cursed. "Warn them off, Davids."

"Transmitting...no response."

"Hopefully they can translate our language."

"Hopefully." O'Brien frowned. "Don't we have some protocol for this?"

"I can transmit computer data with a language database...they should be able to interpret it in time."

"Do it."

"And then we wait?"

"I don't have a lot of patience."

"*Ryu-Chi* is moving."

"What?' O'Brien looked at the display. "Attack vector?"

"Not towards us."

"What the hell are they doing?"

"*Ryu-chi* is firing!"

"Damn them!" O'Brien cursed. "Gun crews, open fire on the *Ryu-Chi*! I won't have those damned Japs trigger an interstellar war."

"Firing now!"

"Energy spike!" Farnsworth shouted. "It's right off the scales, Major..."

"Goddamn." O'Brien stared at the visual image.

The *Ryu-Chi* was drifting, most of its forward structure in half-melted ruins. A second barrage of blue-coloured energy bolts lashed at the Human warship.

"What kind of weapon was that?"

"I'm not sure."

"They don't look like lasers?" Piotrowski asked. "Particle beams?"

"Not like any we have. I'm not sure what that was."

"Comms are taking static...looks like a low-level electromagnetic pulse. I'm attempting to compensate."

"*Hachiman* and *Bishamon* are moving on intercept vectors," Farnsworth called out.

"Damn them! Gun crews, lock and—"

"The intruder is targeting the *Roosevelt*."

"Whose side is that bastard on?"

"*Roosevelt* has been hit. She's drifting, Major."

"That does it. Order to all batteries. Lock onto the Intruder and blast it into scrap. We'll sort through the wreckage later."

"Delta batteries on-line. Firing laser Delta-Two."

Piotrowski was bent over the sensor station. "Direct hit...not sure if we caused any damage."

"We hit them...we must have caused *some* damage."

"Energy spike!"

"Brace for impact!" the major shouted.

The station rocked. Its rotation faltered and for several long moments, there was no gravity.

The lights dimmed and systems all over the command deck flickered.

"What the hell hit us?" O'Brien wiped blood from a cut on his forehead. "Sit-rep!"

"Some kind of electromagnetic weapon." The station's rotation was picking up speed and the gravity was slowly returning to normal levels. "More powerful than anything I've ever seen, Sir."

"Power failures in the outer decks. Delta Section is reporting widespread malfunctions and system failures."

"Delta batteries are off-line!"

O'Brien took a breath. "Stand by for another attack."

Piotrowski cursed. "The Intruder is firing on the *Hachiman*."

"Looks like an interesting vid."

"Historical." Arden turned his head away from the monitor. "Welcome back, Captain Zane."

"I wish it was under a better circumstances, Admiral."

"So do I. The loss of Moria will be sorely felt."

Zane winced. "I did my best. The Devastators won the system, but it cost them heavily."

"I have no doubt of that. I've already skimmed your debriefing. You have nothing to be ashamed of...the odds were badly stacked against you." Arden turned back towards the vid-projector. "This is first contact at LaGrange Three. June of Twenty-One Eleven."

"Ah. O'Brien's command."

"That's the one. The Ospma had been watching us for decades...they had our system mapped thoroughly. That wormhole opened right near LaGrange Three and a *Warsphere* popped out."

"And O'Brien tried to destroy it."

"Only after they'd targeted him first...which was after the Japanese opened fire. What a mess that made for the politicians." *The two sides probably would have started World War Three if the Ospma hadn't arrived.* "The Ospma disabled Liberty Station with a single volley from their surge cannons." A smile pulled at Arden's mouth. "He was lucky they only used surge cannons...a few volleys from their electromagnetic bolters or resonance generators would have done a lot worse."

"It was a pretty damned good gesture for first contact."

"It got the results the Ospma wanted. We stopped fighting each other and listened to them."

"They got what they wanted." Zane gestured towards the frozen display. "They demonstrated their superiority over us and we agreed to become their allies."

"They gave us the stars."

"Yes, but they led us into war with the Devastators."

"It's quite possible, and probable, that the Devastators would have found us first."

"Is that your opinion?"

"Yes, it is." Arden nodded his head. He picked up his coffee mug from the desk and took a drink. "And, without Ospma technological support, we would have stood no chance against the Devastators."

"Even with their support, we don't stand much chance."

"Moria could not have been held."

"Where was Sixth Fleet?"

"On other duties."

"There was only one factory ship. With Sixth Fleet, we could have won."

"You don't know that for sure."

"No..." Zane was forced to admit. "But I might not have had to leave so many civilians behind either."

Chapter Four

Zane paced slowly along the hallway. He had been assigned temporary quarters on the third floor of the Complex. "I really don't want to be here," he grumbled. His boots clicked loudly on the floor tiles and his dark blue jacket and pants—standard Spacey uniform—seemed out of place with the grandeur of the sixth floor.

"Why not?" Kathleen Levy smiled at him with delighted amusement. Her own elegant pumps made no sound as she walked through the hallway. "You've been assigned beautiful quarters. They must be a lot nicer than anything you'd get assigned to in the military."

"I'm used to the military. I'm not used to this." He gestured to the carved wood paneling and plant-filled alcoves which they were passing. "I guess that it's just not Spartan enough for me. Even the third floor is—"

"Not Spartan enough for you?" Levy shrugged. Her dark green skirt and vest were strictly businesslike, but she wore a red blouse more fiery than her hair. "The third floor is fairly sedate compared to the rich luxuries of the fifth and higher floors," she said. "I thought *they* certainly would be too rich for you." Then she laughed softly at his startled expression. "I am certain that you are just not ready for the luxury of the ninth floor."

Zane gave his head a rueful shook his head. "I'm just a captain, not a politician." The ninth level was where the top government officials lived, along with admirals, generals, and the Joint Chiefs.

"You're a hero."

He snorted.

Two Asian women walked past, talking together so rapidly in Japanese that neither paid any attention to either Zane or Levy.

Zane glanced over his shoulder at them.

"You are in the very heart of EarthGov." Kathleen patted his arm. "Here a ship's captain is of no great importance."

"Thanks."

"Well, I know that on your own ship, you're used to being treated like God."

"On any Spacey ship, the captain is God."

"Like the Navy?"

"Just like in the wet navy," Zane agreed. "Army, Navy, Spacey...the defenders of the Human Worlds."

They stepped around a corner and into a comfortable lounge. One entire wall was open to the Green Well and plants clustered thickly around the balcony. The air was heavy with the scent of flowers.

"I love this level...so many nice places just to stop and talk."

Zane sneezed. *Must be whatever is growing in here.* "I don't have a lot of time for your tour, Kathleen. I have to get to the military wing. I have a meeting with Colonel Lawrence."

Kathleen nodded. "I should go and attend to my own business before the next Parliamentary session begins." She pulled a small *Transcom P2050* comp-pad from a pocket inside her jacket and checked it. "Yes, the next session should be starting shortly. Beth will have a fit if I'm late." She stuffed the pad back into her pocket. "Damn. I was just starting to enjoy myself."

So am I, Zane thought. And he was surprised by that. "At least we can we can share the tram there."

"Yes, we do have that. Come on."

The tram station was crowded with diplomats and their aides waiting for the next empty seat. The tram followed a set network around the perimeter of the Complex with numerous stations. Given the size of the complex, the trams were a very popular means of traveling between sections.

Kathleen paused to exchange greetings with a couple of aides she knew. She introduced Zane to them both.

Not knowing what to say, Zane was relieved when an empty tram arrived at the station. He quickly took a seat.

Kathleen Levy sat down beside him. "It's a nice way to travel."

"It's a sign that this complex is too large." Zane shook his head. "You need to ride a train to travel between the wings."

"The Government has a number of bureaucracies."

"Too many."

"They need them to operate. The United Human Worlds still covers a lot of territory, Zane."

"I would never have known that," he replied dryly. "I only fly through most of it every day."

"You military types." She shook her head.

The tram pulled around a corner and slowed to a stop.

Zane had lost track of the number of stops the tram had made so far—he thought this was the sixteenth or seventeenth.

"This is my stop." In a single graceful motion, Kathleen rose to her feet. "Goodbye, Zane." She leaned in close and gave him a kiss on his left cheek. "See you tonight, right?"

"Of course. Dinner at the usual place?"

"Always. Bye!" She hurried off into the Great Hall, towards the Parliament Chamber.

Zane stared after her, but she was quickly swallowed up in the milling crowds.

The Hall was ornate and opulent—and he knew that the Chamber was even more so. Marble pillars rose ten metres up to support the vaulted ceiling and murals covered the walls. Scores of lesser corridors branched off from the Hall, leading to offices and lounges and cafeterias and all the other places necessary to maintain the smooth functioning of government.

Members of Parliament milled around in soft conversations and aides circled them like planetary bodies.

Sentries stood at various points, wearing polished body armour and ceremonial weaponry. They were clearly meant to be more decorative than effective.

Zane shook his head as the tram back lurched into motion.

* * *

By contrast, the office level was considerably less ornate. The corridor was still tiled, but there were a lot fewer statues and plants in evidence. There were also marines standing on guard duty near the tram stations and elevators. The manner in which they held their weaponry left no doubt that they were not meant to be strictly decorative.

Zane was the only person to get off the tram at this particular station. Of course, by now he was also one of the few passengers left.

Zane allowed his ident-card to be examined by two gray-uniformed members of security. *I smell fish,* he thought while they checked his DNA with a portable scanner. *Must be an Ospma nearby.*

"You may proceed," the taller of them said.

"Thank you." Zane stepped through the checkpoint. He wasn't wearing his side arm, so he wondered if he would have been allowed to keep it. *No way too tell without actually wearing it here sometime, I suppose.*

"A lot of bother, eh?"

"You said it." Zane turned his head towards the speaker. He didn't recognize the slender man.

"Captain Zane?"

"Yes?"

"Nathan Fisk." The slender man offered his hand. "I've been waiting for you."

"Sorry, I didn't think I was that late."

"Oh, you're not." Fisk wore a dark blue uniform with insignia and rank pins. "I just like to be early for things."

Zane's eyes rested briefly on particular pin. "P.O.B.?" he asked, his eyes narrowing.

Fisk nodded. "Yes, I'm with the Psionic Oversight Bureau."

"I didn't know Colonel Lawrence had a telepath for an aide."

"We *are* everywhere, you know." Fisk grinned at his joke on the current advertisement campaign. "This way, please." He led the way down one of the many hallways.

Zane glanced idly at the office doors they were passing. Most didn't have nameplates on them, only numbers. *How do you know which one is right?* He didn't see many people in this particular hallway either. "Are there many psions around?"

"No, Captain. Not very many of us have been assigned as governmental attaches as yet. We're still very much a misunderstood branch. No one is sure if we're going to be strictly a military asset."

"I see. I guess I never really—"

"Thought about it before?" Fisk's grin was quite wide. "Most people have never even heard of the P.O.B., even with the current advertising campaign. Most people who know about psions think of us as mind reading freaks." There was a hint of bitterness in his voice. "We're hoping we can change that attitude."

"I haven't interacted with any psions before." Zane licked his lips. "I didn't mean to offend you."

"You didn't. Offend me that is." Fisk gave him a friendly smile. "You're leaking, Captain."

"What?"

"Your thoughts are leaking all over." The telepath chuckled, his laughter growing as Zane looked more confused. "It's refreshing actually."

"It is?"

"I deal with politicians almost every day. Political and military ones. You have a very straightforward mind. Nice and ordered thoughts—not that I mean to pry, of course, but you are broadcasting them loudly—and you mean exactly what you say."

"Unlike politicians."

"Exactly." Fisk stopped outside of one door. "You can go right in. He's expecting you."

"Thank you." Zane shook Fisk's hand, and then he opened the door and stepped into an office and froze.

Gareth Jarrell, commanding officer of First Fleet, was sitting at the small desk and studying a computer display. "Do come in, Captain." He had a strong English accent from his childhood in Manchester.

"Admiral." Zane barely managed to keep his voice smooth. The door closed behind him, with Nathan Fisk still outside.

"Yes, it's not my usual office. Sometimes it's good to come down and work amongst the regular staff. Puts the fear of God into them." His lips twitched into a sharp smile. "Makes it harder for the other Joint Chiefs to find you too."

What is going on? Zane wondered. "I was expecting to meet with Colonel Lawrence."

Jarrell shook his head. "Benjamin was reassigned. Rather suddenly, I might add."

"Oh."

"You sound relieved."

"Who ever looks forward to a meeting with Internal Affairs? Sir," he added hastily."

"True enough." Jarrell turned back to his keyboard and typed a command into it with one hand.

A map flashed across one of the wall-mounted screen.

Zane recognized it easily enough. "Earth."

"And its local holdings." Jarrell gestured. "Earth, Mars Colony, Venus Habitat, Io Outpost, Ganymede Station, Saturn Station. To say nothing of the various asteroid mining colonies or the LaGrange habitats. All in all, Captain, one of the most heavily inhabited systems in the known galaxy."

"The Sol System is the heart of the United Human Worlds. It stands to reason that we would have the largest concentration of colonies here." Zane knew all that. *What are you getting at?*

"The Sol System remains a vital one. First Fleet is based here, with the full support of one of the strongest defensive fortification networks in the galaxy. This is *the* one system that Humanity cannot afford to lose."

"Why tell me?"

Jarrell stared coldly at him.

"I'm just a fleet captain, not a member of the Joint Chiefs."

"I have your file, Captain. I've been reading it." Jarrell gave him a cold studying look. "You are a captain in the Expeditionary Fleet. You tend to be more...independent than most captains. You're out in the field far more often than you are at a home port."

"I like serving as the Spacey requires."

"You excel at defending the colonies."

Zane grimaced. "And watching colonies fall."

"Moria was a small loss."

Zane's eyes narrowed in surprise.

Jarrell nodded his head. "In the grand scheme, preserving the bulk of Sixth Fleet to defend the rest of the sector was necessary. Lives were lost, true, but more lives can be saved in the long run."

Zane shook his head. *I don't know about that. How many worlds can we write off in the name of 'the long run'?* "So why call me here?"

"Because you have seen the Devastators first hand. You have fought them. If they come here, we have to stop them. Without losing *any* more of our colonies."

Zane started to nod his agreement, and then he froze, feeling a sudden chill. "If the Devastators get loose around Earth...."

"They'd level the planet."

"You're a Fleet Admiral. You can muster the entire First Fleet here if you need too." Zane paused, still feeling that chill. "Do you need too?"

"I hope not."

Chapter Five

"Red sky at night, shepherds delight; red sky in the morning, sailors take warning."

"What was that, Sir?"

Michael Spencer shook his head. "Nothing, Dwayne. Just an old rhyme my granny used to tell me." The captain was staring at a display showing the mottled reddish sky of hyperspace. The *Tengu King* was holding station in that disconcerting dimension along with other elements from the newly commissioned Sixth Fleet, waiting to transit into the star system that the United Human Worlds had named Beta Durani.

"Captain Spencer?"

He turned his head towards the crewman who had just called out his name. "Yes, Lieutenant Pickman?"

"We have an update from our recon probes...energy emissions detected near asteroid cluster Pegasus three nine seven."

"Understood." Michael Spencer leaned back in his chair. "Rogers, is there any comment from the Ospma?"

The blonde communications officer shook her head. "Negative. Every channel is quiet."

Spencer looked out into hyperspace again. The mottled red sky was still bloody. *And it's just breaking dawn at Syra Planum,* he thought after a glance at his watch.

"My grandson is celebrating his first birthday today." Spencer looked at his first officer. "What kind of universe is Jeffrey going to grow up in?" he asked with resignation heavy in his voice.

Dwayne Leftcourt shrugged. "A galaxy at war it seems."

"That is my greatest fear." Spencer took a breath, knowing that he could wait no longer. "Contact the Ospma...Sixth Fleet is ready to engage."

The squadron emerged from the swirling whirlpool.

I wish we had the ability to open wormholes from our starships, Spencer thought with more than a trace of jealously. Not even his *Deliverance*-class cruiser had enough raw power to do so. *Our allies guard that technology very closely.* Along with all access to the mysterious and hyper-rare elements which were a key component in constructing worm-engines. *Of course, even the Ospma only integrate worm-engines into a handful of their designs.* The rarity could be a deadly weakness in battle—if the *Scout Wheel* or *Warsphere* was destroyed, then any fleet survivors would be cut off and trapped.

"*Beholder* is moving off," Dan Pickman announced."

Spencer had expected that. Even with eight surge cannons and four electro-magentic pulsars, the *Scout Wheel* was far too valuable to risk in pitched combat because of its integral worm-engine. *One of the only ship types built with worm-engines.* "Begin shunting power to our weaponry."

"Copy that."

The captain listened to the soft background sounds of his ship. He could tell a surprising number of details about how well the *Tengu King* was operating from just listening to the ambient noise.

"Visual contact!" Pickman called out. "Three alien craft detected, moving towards the asteroid cluster."

Spencer looked at the icons. "Identify them." They were well beyond his fleet's weapons' range.

"Scanning now."

"Shunt additional power to the sensor array," Leftcourt ordered.

"Aye, Sir." The extra power would help with the identification of the ships. "They're moving into the asteroid rings."

Spencer grimaced. "A good place...the debris will mask them from us." The aliens could stay hidden there for some time and the Earth ships would have to go in hunting. *Right into a nice little ambush if there are more of them already hidden inside that cluster.*

"Incoming transmission from the *Beholder*...commence attack."

"Open a channel, full protocols." Spencer kept his voice calm, though his mouth twisted at the peremptory way in which the Ospma commanded him to attack. "Standard languages." He paused for a moment longer, until Beth Rogers looked back at him and nodded her head. "This is Captain Michael Spencer, UHW *Spacey*. This star system is claimed under Earth jurisdiction as one of its possessions. Withdraw at once." It wasn't a lie either. The United Human Worlds did claim the system and the Ospma had ceded it to them. *Now we just have to secure it from the pirates the Ospma told us about.*

"No response."

"Repeat the signal."

She shook her head. "Still no response from the aliens."

Spencer just managed to suppress his sigh. *I hoped we could do this through diplomacy,* he thought to himself. *I don't want to be the first Human captain to declare war on an alien race.*

"We have another attack order coming in from the *Beholder*."

"Acknowledge it, but inform the *Beholder* that I'm not opening fire until we have properly identified the enemy." Spencer didn't bother to mask the irritation he felt at the Ospma's attitudes. *They do like to boss us around. This is supposed to be an equal partnership between us. I wonder if they know that.* "Maintain our position and continue hailing the aliens."

"Aye, Sir."

"The Ospma won't like this." Leftcourt kept his voice soft. "They've issued their orders."

"It's our comm-system that we're using, not theirs."

"Aye, Sir."

Spencer looked at his first officer with a rueful smile. "Sixth Fleet, such as it currently is, is my command...the Ospma will have to wait until I choose to commit my ships."

Dwayne Leftcourt nodded his head in agreement. "You have our support, Captain."

"Enemy ships leaving the asteroid cluster..."

Michael Spencer smiled in relief at the report. *Finally. It's been a very long four hours.* "Then, Pickman, you should finally be able to get a clear scan of them."

The sensor officer smiled at the gentle teasing. "Aye, Sir." He bent over his console, typing in a series of commands and then checking the sensor feeds. "Silhouettes are confirmed...the war-book calls them *Blackbeard* attack frigates." The elegant-looking ships pictured on the displays had stubby central cores with forward curving wings. "Eight of them."

"Threat assessment, Lieutenant Leftcourt?"

"Assuming they follow standard Goolatch designs, then they'll be armed with a plasma cannon and two particle beams. Class-five sensors and class-eight engines." Leftcourt had already studied the war-book entry. "Small swift ships. Decent firepower for their size, but not enough mass or structure to survive many hard hits."

Spencer could guess at the tactics soon to be employed by those eight ships. "Repeated fast attacks by light ships to wear us down."

"Should we alter our course, Captain?"

"No, Martini, hold formation. Transfer power to weapon batteries." He had three *Deliverance* cruisers—each armed with two missile racks, seven surge cannons, plus four interceptor grids—as well as two *Torrential* missile cruisers under his command. *Not counting the Ospma in reserve.* "Let them come to us."

"All units are standing by." Leftcourt hastily checked his seat restraints. "Sixth Fleet is ready to engage."

"Warn them off one last time." Spencer studied the ships as they closed. *Two distinct wolf packs*, he noted from their formations. "Are they official Goolatch Royal Navy or just pirates?"

"No way to tell, Sir. Not unless they want to tell us."

"I don't want to provoke a war by firing on legitimate naval units."

"The Ospma said they were pirates."

Spencer lowered his voice. "How much do you trust everything the Ospma tell us?" he asked.

Leftcourt grimaced.

Spencer nodded. "Exactly." He raised his voice. "Take us ahead at half-speed, and then alert Captain Hiroshi to ready his first volley."

"Aye, Captain." Adriano Martini licked his lips. "Accelerating to half-speed."

Spencer watched the displays carefully. The two *Torrential* cruisers held station relative on the flagship as it began to move. The *Blackbeards* were still closing. Then both *Torrentials* launched eight missiles towards the incoming Goolatch.

Explosions blossomed from two of the lead *Blackbeard* frigates.

"Direct hits on targets," Pickman reported. "Ships are falling out of formation. One wolf pack is scattering."

"Where is the second pack?"

"Incoming!"

The *Tengu King* shuddered as a burst of superheated plasma burned into its hull.

"Direct hit!"

"Return fire!" Spencer shouted over the wail of alarms. "The second pack is coming around again." *And the first one must be regrouping.* "Communication intercepts?"

"Negative. Signals are heavily encrypted."

"Record everything, Rogers. We'll let the Eyes read it later."

Leftcourt was snapping orders to his gunners. "Surge cannons are firing as fast as they can recharge...that plasma cannnon out-ranges us."

"Maintain firing rate."

"*Daikyu* is launching again. Missiles bearing on target."

One of the other *Deliverances* had broken formation was burning towards the asteroid cluster at high speed.

"*Oni* is moving to sweep the cluster."

"Continue firing all batteries." Spencer cursed under his breath. Those *Blackbeards* were tough little ships, racing in to snap off quick shots at his cruisers. *Sound tactics. These Goolatch are tough for pirates.*

One of the *Torrential* cruisers flushed its racks and two more of the *Blackbeards* succumbed to damage and drifted away from the battle.

"There's another ship leaving the asteroid cluster."

"Goolatch?"

"Warbook calls it a *Nalor* cruiser." Leftcourt adjusted his monitor to better view the sensor display. "Five plasma cannon of varying weights, particle cannons, class-eight sensors, class-nine engine."

"Fast and tough."

"Aye, Captain." Leftcourt nodded. "*Oni* is still advancing."

Spencer eyed the silhouette of the Goolatch warship. *Looks like a scaled up version of the Blackbeard. I hope it's the only one they have.* "What's its course?"

"Right towards us."

Spencer nodded his head. "Of course it would be coming this way."

"The *Beholder* is holding station with its own escorts."

Well clear of the battle, of course. They want to watch the show, but not interfere. Unless it's in their best interest of course. "Is the *Beholder's* worm-engine recharged?"

"Negative."

"Then we fight." The light escorts would be useful in this growing battle, but he wasn't about to ask for them. *I won't give the Ospma the satisfaction. We can handle this ourselves. I hope.*

"*Nalor* is still closing. *Oni* is altering course to intercept."

They won't make it in time. Spencer grimaced. "Leftcourt, give the *Nalor* a volley of surge cannons."

"Firing now!"

"Energy spike!" Pickman shouted. "They're firing on *Daikyu!*"

"Damn it!"

Daikyu was hit hard.

Plasma burned through its armoured hull and then the *Nalor's* particle beams lanced into the still-sparking craters. A moment later, powerful internal exploisons tore through the cruiser, scattered hull plates and other equipment into space.

"Massive energy spikes," Pickman reported in a quiet voice. "The Goolatch must have hit a magazine."

"Damn." Spencer winced as the boxy *Torrential* blew itself apart. "Launch shuttles and search for survivors." *Some of the crew must have gotten to the lifepods. UHW Spacey ships were designed for optimum crew survival in any situation.*

"Goolatch are closing."

Spencer bared his teeth. "Hit them back." He grunted as the surge canons fired and the charged energy particles slammed into the *Nalor.*

Explosions gutted one of the forward weapon mounts.

"Martini, go evasive!"

"Aye, Captain."

"Leftcourt, try to hit their reactors. Shut them down if you can." *The better to disable and capture new technology we can reverse-engineer.* Spencer wondered if the Ospma would allow them to salvage the Goolatch wreckage. *Or will* they *destroy the hulks to prevent us from gaining any new technologies?*

"Aye, Captain. Firing surge cannons."

The bursts looked good as they splashed against the brightly painted hull.

"Multiple hits on the *Nalor.* Heavy damage."

"Good shooting." Spencer had felt his own ship take hits. "What's our status?"

"Minor breaches to the port hull. Internal bulkheads have sealed. Repair crews are responding."

"Captain, the Goolatch are retreating."

"Are they?" Spencer was surprised. *It was a close thing. A bit more pushing and they might have won the battle.*

Pickman turned his head to look at the captain. "Their remaining ships are heading out-system at high speed."

Spencer frowned at that. "We detected no space stations. Do their ships have worm-engines?"

"Not reading any such emissions, Captain." Pickman shook his head. Worm-engines gave off a particular energy signal when active.

"So they can't open a wormhole?"

"No, Sir."

"Then why try running?" Leftcourt asked. "They might be able to keep out of weapons range, but we can still track them."

Spencer frowned as well. "Rogers, contact the *Beholder*. Ask if they've detected any other ships."

"No response from the Ospma."

"None?"

"Captain, look!"

The *Scout Wheel* had moved towards the battlefield with its escorts and now the Ospma were firing on the Goolatch wreckage. New explosions were erupting from the debris.

"Warn them off!" Spencer ordered in outrage as the largest piece of *Blackbeard* wreckage exploded.

"No response." Roger continued typing in commands. "Not on any frequencies."

"Damn them!" Spencer slammed his fist onto the arm of his chair. "Damn them!" *So much for salvage.* "Launch our remaining shuttles. Send them in to check the Goolatch wreckage for survivors."

"Aye, Captain."

"What about the *Beholder*?"

"Open signal...we are sending in rescue teams. If the Ospma fire on *any* of our ships or shuttles, we *will* return fire." Spencer's voice was like iron. "I do not condone firing on helpless crewers."

"Aye, Captain." Rogers swallowed hard, then turned to transmit the message.

Leftcourt whistled softly. "EarthGov won't be too happy about this."

"Let them complain. They promoted me to command this fleet. And, by God, I will command it in my own way."

The *Tengu King's* shuttle bay was crowded with two shuttles landed and the disembarking crews.

Michael Spencer eyed the aliens being helped off his shuttles. They were Human-size, with faces covered with short, curly fur.

One of the prisoners had a particularly tall and spiky mane. His clothing was fairly ornate, with more trim and braid than Spencer had seen on anyone other than portraits of Renaissance-era French nobility. He stepped closer to the alien. "Is he all right, Doctor Pulaski?"

The doctor shook her head and grimaced. She was holding a portable scanner—an Ospma invention—in her right hand. "Internal injuries. Smoke inhalation. With so much of his physiology a mystery, I don't think I can save him."

Spencer winced. "Do your best."

"Do I ever not?"

The Goolatch coughed fitfully as he was laid on a stretcher. "Can't win...every battle."

Spencer blinked in surprise. *He speaks Ospma?* Or at least as well as a Human could pronounce that particular language. *Different vocal apparatus, differently breathing abilities as well.* "Are you the captain?"

"Maldoona...Kiro."

"Michael Spencer. We are attempting to rescue as many survivors as we can. You will be returned to your people."

"Have no...people. No importance."

"You were willing to fight and die for a star system. Surely you have importance." Spencer's eyes narrowed. "Unless you really are the pirates the Ospma claim you people are."

Kiro smiled and closed his eyes.

"What made this system so valuable?" Spencer demanded.

The Goolatch opened his eyes and then he laughed, gasping for breath as he did so. "You have...no idea why...you...fight?" He coughed. "Foolish slaves. Fools."

"What about your survivors? They can't escape to hyperspace."

"A *Strela*...is waiting. Can't catch...."

"*Strela*? What's a *Strela*? A ship of some kind?"

Pulaski shook her head. "He's unconscious."

"Take him to med bay then. Do what you can."

She was still grimacing.

Chapter Six

"I've seen shuttles carrying a number of the Joint Chiefs...this must be an important meeting."

"It is, Corwin." Dale Arden nodded and checked the small computer pad. "This promises to be a very important meeting indeed." He let his gaze drift around the room. It was a fairly small conference room, actually, dominated by an oval table. *Oak, I think it is.* Computer keypads had been inlaid into the table's surface, to upgrade it to the modern era of course.

The door hissed open and a tall, slender, blonde woman stepped through. She gave the room a quick glance, and then her green eyes lit up. "Dale." She hurriedly walked across the floor to his side.

"Sabrina." He gave her a hug. "I'm glad to see you made it."

"I can't spend all of my time over at Wolf." She gave him a shrug. "However much I'd like too."

"I know the feeling."

"I should be going, Admiral." Corwin offered Sabrina a salute, then hurried towards the doorway.

"Admiral Arden. Admiral Webber." The new arrival was shorter than either of them, with dark hair and brown eyes. The dark colours of his uniform went well with his dusky skin tone.

Sabrina gave him a cool nod. "Admiral Singh."

Ashvim Singh smiled back quite warmly—as if to mock her own forced greeting. "You are doing fine work at Wolf." He spoke the words with false charm heavy in his voice. "The shipyards there have never been more efficiently run."

"Thank you. I do my best to strengthen the United Human Worlds."

"Hopefully the others will soon agree with me that we need to take full advantage of the Fleet's strength." He nodded towards Arden. "The galaxy contains many threats, not just the Devastators."

"As you say," Arden replied. "But sometimes merely having strength of arms is insufficient to win a war."

Singh frowned.

"History has many examples of a small group outfighting a much larger national army."

"Yes, of course." Singh seemed off-balance now.

Sabrina turned her head to try and hide her sudden smile at Singh's sudden discomfort.

"If you will excuse me?" Singh hurried towards the oak table and fell into conversation with Vanya Ivanova and Moira Wassen, the commanding officers of Second and Third Fleets.

"I don't like him." Sabrina shook her head. "I really do not like him."

"Singh is one of the dominant powers within UHW Spacey. He has ambition and a driving hunger for power."

"Not a good combination."

Arden nodded his agreement.

"Coldly charming. A calculating and precise thinker." Lee Hwan Kim's eyes were tracking Singh like a missile lock. "He could be a complete disaster for the United Human Worlds if he ever became head of the Joint Chiefs."

"That seems unlikely," Arden pointed out softly. "He lacks the political support to carry a majority."

"For now."

"You would know," Arden agreed. *Military Intelligence is firmly under your sway.*

Kim nodded his head rather sadly.

The door opened and several officers entered *en masse.*

Garik Kopinksi was the first in, followed by Jennifer Romano, Gareth Jarrell, and Dwayne Leftcourt. Jarrell was talking rapidly to the commander of Seventh Fleet and Leftcourt was listening with a bored expression on his thin face.

"Kopinksi looks worn," Sabrina commented in a low tone.

Arden nodded. "The last few weeks have been trying for Garik." *He was not aging well at all. His hair is graying so fast.*

"So I heard."

"The war is very tiring."

Sabrina Webber gave a sigh. "I hate admitting this, even just to you, but Singh might be right. We need to change the status quo."

Arden looked surprised for a moment. "I did not expect to hear you—" he broke off as the door opened and Prime Minister Trudeau entered the room at last.

"Sorry to be late, ladies and gentlemen." Trudeau hurried to his chair at the assumed head of the table and sat down. "The Parliament session ran over with the debate."

"Fallout from Moria?" Kim asked as the Joint Chiefs took their own chairs.

Trudeau grimaced in response.

Arden reached for the pale green glass in front of him, wishing vaguely that it held something stronger than mere water.

"We should not waste any more time." Trudeau eyed each of his top officers in turn. "What is the status of the Sixth Fleet?"

Kopinski started. "With the fall of Moria, Regula has been virtually cut off from the rest of the United Human Worlds. I am gathering all of my available ships at Kapteyn."

"You're going to abandon the rest of the sector?"

Admiral Kopinski shook his head. "No, Prime Minister, but I need to safeguard what colonies I can. An attack against Earth is coming...every one of us knows that." He shook his head as no one else spoke up. "I have to safeguard the hyperspace beacon route out of my sector. Kapteyn will be the next logical target."

"The Devastators have not shown any reliance on the beacons. They travel through hyperspace at random and attack at will. They could strike anywhere."

"Always the alarmist, Jarrell?" Singh chuckled. "Most of their attacks occur along beacon networks."

Sabrina Webber shook her head. "But not all of them do."

"Enough of them do." Singh waved his hand. "The other attacks are simply to distract us from strongly fortifying our border worlds. They are trying to keep us off-balance."

Arden nodded. "The strategy is working."

"Every known star-faring race relies on the beacon network," Singh reminded them. "To leave the network is too risk becoming lost in hyperspace. Only dedicated exploration ships take that chance."

"Only dedicated explorers have the sensor suites necessary to scan for planetary gravity shadows in hyperspace. And only a handful of ships can open wormholes back into normal space." Kopinksi was stating the obvious.

"To slow the advance, we need to change the network."

All eyes were focused on Singh.

"You can't be serious!" Vanya Ivanova spoke up for the first time. "You want us to cut the beacons?"

"Yes."

"We can't sever all of the beacons. *We'd* be cut off."

"We don't have much choice, Sabrina."

"We don't have many colonies left to travel too." Arden took another drink from his water glass. "Or do you propose to simply isolate the UHW from the rest of the galaxy?"

Singh glared at him.

Jennifer Romano shook her head. "The Fleet can't hold the Devastators off. It's been proven time after time, in battle after battle. What other option does that leave us?"

Trudeau looked at her. "You want more funding for your ground forces then?"

"Doesn't everyone?" Romano laughed, though without very much real amusement. "The Fleet cannot adequately defend our colonies...why not increase our ground forces?"

"Because the Devastators do not bother with ground assaults." Singh barely managed to sound civil. "They blast anything strategic from orbit and then vacuum up the debris for processing. Additional ground troops would be a complete waste."

"Of lives?" Trudeau asked.

"Yes," Singh replied after a long moment.

There was a moment of silence.

Anton Trudeau exchanged looks with Singh and then Arden. He managed not to sigh aloud and looked across the table. "Sabrina, what news do you have about starfighter development?"

"Still nothing worthwhile to report. R&D is having difficulty producing a fusion reactor compact enough to fit within the hull of a starfighter." She offered a shrug. "We just don't have the expertise."

"What about Ospma assistance?" Jarrell asked. "We desperately need a fighter design to interdict those drone swarms."

"R&D have been working on starfighter designs for centuries. We just can't produce an acceptable power plant."

"R&D's excuses are wearing thin."

William Hague frowned at Singh's tone.

"We have numerous power plants available, do we not?"

Sabrina shook her head. "Ospma singularities are simply too big, Ganya. They are just not suitable for use in anything smaller than a shuttle. Any of our own reactors, at that size, are not powerful enough to provide a fighter with necessary speed or maneuverability."

Singh grimaced. "This remains unacceptable. The Fleet needs a fighter to engage the Devastator drones."

"It should be a simple matter to reverse-engineer one of *their* power plants. We *have* salvaged enough drones after recent battles."

"Oh, we can certainly reproduce their reactors, Prime Minister," Sabrina agreed, "almost in the correct size for a fighter fuselage. Unfortunately the radiation levels those ion engines emit is *lethal*. Any pilot would die before completing his first mission."

Singh snorted.

"Research will continue. Some new shielding for the engines perhaps. I have considerable confidence in my technical staff."

"Perhaps those researches will bear fruit." Trudeau took a drink from his glass. "Admiral Hague?"

William Hague ran a hand through his beard before answering. "The battles progress. We have defences in place, but we can only do what we can. The war continues."

"The war always continues, Hague. We need to change the course of the war."

"What about our attempts at finding new allies?"

"Other than the Ospma?" Hague asked.

"Yes."

Leftcourt shook his head. "Not much luck of that. The Ospma keep us on a tight leash."

"True."

"We can't travel far without a beacon to lock onto and the Ospma keep access to the most distant beacons restricted." Leftcourt commanded the Seventh Fleet—the one dedicated to permanent duty in the Ospma Baronies. "I have orders for my captains to make contact with other species, but we've only engaged a few pirates and bandits. They shoot first and don't talk, even after being taken as prisoners."

Hague sighed. "Sometimes I think that the Devastators have wiped out every other species."

"We don't have the resources to send ships beyond United Human Worlds-Barony space." Singh made that comment. "Every ship is needed to defend our remaining colonies." His lips twitched into a smile. "A further expansion of the UHW Spacey fleet would be of some help. Should we wish to divert ships into wasteful missions—"

"Admiral, if explorers were able to discover a powerful race who could be convinced to join the war against the Devastators, then it would not be a waste."

"If there are powerful races out there, Vanya, then why aren't they already fighting?"

"They might be defending their own territories."

"In which case why would they wish to come and rescue us?" Singh paused a moment. "What if these mythical saviors drove off the Devastators and then annexed the United Human Worlds for themselves?"

"I'd rather risk possible slavery than outright destruction."

Singh stared at Marc Gascoigne with narrow eyes. "Would you gamble the United Human Worlds against such a chance?" He shook his head. "Too risky."

"There is no evidence than another race would seek to conquer us." Arden kept his voice steady. "Rumours about the Goolatch and Raptchi notwithstanding. We need to find allies."

"We already have the Ospma."

"The Ospma cannot help us...we are losing the war." Ivanova kept his voice steady. "We must do something."

"Such as?" Trudeau waited. "The United Human Worlds are dying." He hated admitting that, but the Joint Chiefs were fully aware of the situation. *They must know the war's progress better than I do.*

Arden nodded his head. "The Devastators are attacking everywhere. *We* can't stop them."

Singh snorted. "And so you would choose to divert resources away from warship construction to exploration ships that you would then send off on blind transits through hyperspace? Madness."

"There are plenty of shipyards we could borrow space from."

"There are no slips to spare, Sabrina."

"There are civilian yards which are unable to produce viable warships," she argued right back. "They could build explorers."

"We lack the funding."

"We can divert funding."

"I do not agree to this plan...at this time."

"Fine." Dale Arden grunted. "Have it your way, Admiral."

Trudeau shook his head. "This is not helping our cause," he said. "We must be *united* for the betterment of mankind. Infighting will only lead to our destruction."

The Joint Chiefs exchanged somewhat sheepish looks.

"Ladies and gentlemen, we must come up with a viable plan to ensure the survival of the Human race." Trudeau continued to stare around the table "We have no other choice."

Chapter Seven

The holographic map of the United Human Worlds hanging over the mahogany desk flickered. Several of the star icons flared, and then one brightened and expanded, replacing the map with the star and planets of a single system.

Collin Zane narrowed his eyes.

"The Devastators are still coming...we've been skirmishing with a recon flotilla near Beta Durani." Dale Arden gestured to the planet's icon with his finger.

"How many ships?"

"A few scouts, carriers, and their drones...so far. We still have a few mining operations there. Not many, of course." Earth-controlled space was contracting as colony after colony fell to the relentless Devastators. "Not anymore."

Zane frowned as he turned his eyes away from the map. "Shouldn't we be sending a battle fleet to assist Admiral Kopinksi in its defence?" He paused, but Arden didn't respond immediately. "Don't we desperately need the resources there?" That colony was a key source of minerals vital for worm-engine construction.

"That is the very same argument which Leftcourt made when we realized there was a renewed offensive underway. The problem is...we have very few ships to spare right now." Arden sighed. "Sixth Fleet is hopelessly overstretched. The Devastators control most of that sector now."

Zane hadn't known that.

"Their carrier-based patrols are everywhere," Arden continued. "Too many of those damned fighter drones swarming every target. Regula has been cut off and Admiral Kopinski is gathering the bulk of his ships at Kapteyn. He plans to try and hold there."

"Parliament should authourize a counterattack."

Arden shook his head. "They don't want to risk diverting more ships to Regula and leaving other systems under defended. That said, we cannot afford to allow the Devastators to continue to operate unmolested. We need the output of the mining operations there to continue expanding the fleet." *Or at least to keep replacing our growing losses.*

Zane nodded. "The quantium-forty is essential to the functioning of worm-gates and worm-engines." He knew that the rare and expensive substance was formed when ordinary matter was subjected to the stresses of a star going nova, pushing some of its electron pair bonds into hyperspace. Although any element could become a quantium, the most commonly-found form was derived from an isotope of potassium with an atomic weight of forty, hence then name *quantium-forty*. "I'll go."

"We've received some data from the few civilian ore barges which have managed to run the blockade. The successful ones, at least."

"How many have been unsuccessful?"

"We don't know." The admiral sighed and slumped into his chair. "We estimate that two out of every five barges manages to escape the system, but we're not sure."

Zane winced.

"They are civilians, with limited sensor suites, but the data has been checked and rechecked." Arden reached for his coffee mug. The brew was bitter on his tongue. "The Devastator patrols are exceedingly heavy. Any squadrons transiting into Beta Durani will be cut to pieces."

"I just need the *Hellstorm*." Zane offered the admiral a feral smile. "And the Devastators won't know what hit them."

After a moment of thought, Arden nodded. "Your ship is currently being resupplied and rearmed. Repairs might take a bit longer, but you should be ready to ship out within the week."

"My crew can use the leave time."

"Sixth Fleet is slated to receive significant reinforcements from the next batch of units nearing completion. They should be launching from the Wolf shipyards inside of three months."

"How many ships?"

"A battle squadron's worth."

"That should make Kopinski happy."

"They were originally slated to join Hague's Fifth Fleet. He won't be happy to lose them."

"No, I imagine not." Zane managed a weak smile at the thought of Hague's expression.

"Dwayne is less pleased at losing you to my machinations."

"I'm willing to serve wherever the Spacey deems me necessary."

"And wherever you can find the most action."

Zane opened his mouth, but closed it again without saying anything.

Arden picked up a comp-pad in his hand and waved it as he spoke. "I've read Admiral Leftcourt's reports on you, Captain. You have a certain recklessness to your command. You're always willing to plunge your ship into the heart of an enemy formation. You always volunteer to lead the charge. A risk-taker."

"If we never take risks, then we'll never have a real chance at winning this war. Sir."

"I do not enjoy sending officers into certain death situations, Zane."

"I don't have any plans to get killed, Admiral."

Arden smiled at the bold statement.

"Everyone knows the risks when they enlist into the UHW Spacey," Zane told him. "I could die just as easily groundside in some freak accident as I could killed in battle. At least this way, I am in command of my own death."

"An interesting way of looking at it." Arden looked down at the *Transcom P2050* in his hand. "I'll sign off on your transfer to my personal command staff. Once the repairs are completed, you will have clearance to proceed to Regula and begin harassment operations."

"I won't let you down."

Arden grimaced, still unhappy with authourizing this attack. "Good luck then, Captain."

"Thank you, Admiral."

* * *

The traffic in the corridor was fairly heavy. Zane made his way through the military personnel and other people. He barely took notice of them, or the Spartan decorations of the seventh level.

"Captain Zane?"

Zane froze in mid-step and turned around. "Yes?"

A UHW Spacey officer hurried along the corridor behind him and slowed to a stop. The man offered a sharp salute. "Felix Boxleitner."

Zane said nothing.

"I've been hoping to run into you," Boxleitner continued. "I've been watching for you."

"And why is that?"

"I was first officer on the *Gorgon* during the raid on Proxima."

Zane's eyes narrowed. "I haven't heard anything about a raid."

"It was classified." Nathan Fisk stepped out from behind a marble pillar, dressed in his usual dark blue uniform. He gave the two startled UHW Spacey officers a smile. "By the personal order of Admiral Singh."

"I see."

"I believe we should continue this interesting conversation outside." Fisk gestured to a doorway under a sign announcing a tram-station. "The Green Well is always a nice setting for personal conversations."

Boxleitner nodded his head. "Sounds good to me." He looked at Zane.

The captain frowned, but as Fisk continued smiling, he finally nodded his own head in agreement. "Very well."

The tram ride back to the front of the Complex had been quiet, due to the presence of so many other passengers. Most of them had been eagerly talking to one another.

Fisk had attempted to start up a conversation several times, but all of his gambits had failed to provoke more than short answers. He finally fell silent, closed his eyes, and appeared to have fallen asleep.

After reaching the station and taking a lift to the ground floor, Zane ignored his companions and concentrated on the smell of plants as they walked along one of the moss paths which wound through the gardens.

This is why I fight, Zane reminded himself as he stared at a marble fountain. *To protect life.* He managed not to laugh aloud at the absurd arrogance of that statement. *Hell, I fight to keep* myself *alive.*

Fisk nodded, more to himself. "We're quite alone, gentlemen. No one else is close enough to overhear us." He smiled. "I'd know."

"Yes, you probably would." Zane paused a moment. "What's your range?"

"Far enough." Fisk patted his jacket. "There are no electronic ears around here either. Surprisingly, the Green Well remains clean of eavesdropping attempts."

"Should we be worried about eavesdropping?"

"No. I've just been around politicians too much." Fisk chuckled. "No doubt everyone has come to some agreement that this particular location will remain neutral and safe for private conversations."

"Fine." Zane turned to the other Spacey officer. "What do you want from me, Boxleitner?"

"A transfer to your ship."

"The *Gorgon* was crippled at Proxima," Fisk explained for him. "Most of the crew were either killed, or else seriously injured. Commander Boxleitner is lucky that he survived."

"A fluke," the officer protested. "Secondary command wasn't touched, but kamikaze drones smashed engineering and took out the bridge. A sheer fluke. We were left drifting while the rest of the battle moved away."

"Left drifting in a powerless hulk," Fisk reminded him. "Isolated in the secondary bridge without power. Most of the *Gorgon* lost even basic life support. That's how most of the crew perished."

Boxleitner had gone pale.

A horrible way to die, Zane thought. "The *Gorgon* was part of First Fleet...why not go through proper channels and arrange a transfer to another ship that way?"

Boxleitner have himself a shake. "Admiral Jarrell is not interested in reassigning officers. Even those without a ship."

Fisk nodded his head, but said nothing.

"Jarrell's been working closely with Singh on some new strategy. There were very few surviving crew members from the *Gorgon's* patrol group. Most were assigned to ground positions or to Singh's personal staff."

"Interesting." Zane could not guess at the plans or reasoning behind most of the admiralty's decisions. *Not even at the best of times.* "Singh has command of overall fleet operations. Why argue with a promotion to ground staff?"

"I want to be in a ship. I don't want a staff position. My place is out there, fighting to protect the United Human Worlds."

Zane turned towards Fisk. "And what is Jarrell's opinion of Boxleitner's request?"

Fisk shrugged. "He offered the commander a position on his staff. Boxleitner refused the offer and now is considered...."

"Ungrateful."

"That as well." Fisk paused a moment, his eyes closed. "It might be best to get him off the planet for a while though. Give the admiral time to forget about him."

"And why choose me?"

"Your reputation as an aggressive officer appeals to me, Captain Zane."

"I already have a first officer."

"Not officially."

Zane turned his heated glare at Boxleitner.

"Gerald Kemp *is* your tactical officer, not your exec."

"Fine, Fisk. I don't see what your concern this is though."

"Call me an interested ally."

"Fine. The *Hellstorm* is shipping out for Beta Durani within the next two days, Commander. If you can cut the transfer orders, you can come along. Otherwise," he shrugged, "you'll just have to find yourself another ship."

"He'll have the transfer orders," Fisk told them. "Courtesy of Admiral Jarrell's office."

"Thank you, Fisk."

"You can owe me a favour, Commander. Try to live long enough for me to collect on it." Fisk gave them a friendly smile. "I have duties to attend too. Good afternoon, gentlemen."

"Thank you, Captain Zane. I look forward to serving with you."

"Say that after we survive Beta Durani." Collin Zane sighed. "Welcome to the *Hellstorm*."

Chapter Eight

"Reports have been coming in for weeks about fresh sightings of Devastators. A sizable fleet seems to be gathering near the frontier." Anton Trudeau stood staring out through his office window at the lush Green Well. "The threat to the United Human Worlds is growing."

"That is only to be expected," Dale Arden commented from his own chair. "We have had such reports for some time. The Devastators are always on the move. UHW Spacey will continue to fight for every system invaded."

"And you're asking me to leave Earth at this time?"

"If you wait for there to be no risk of attacks by the Devastators, then you would never leave Earth."

"And the problem with that would be what?" Trudeau asked, only half-joking. He left the window and paced across the carpeting. "I need a drink before we continue this conversation."

"All that being said," Cynthia Randall offered from her chair, "our scouts indicate the hyperspace beacon route is still clear for your journey, Prime Minister. It promises to be historic."

Trudeau grimaced at his press secretary's words, and then shook his head. "I have little desire to travel off-world right now. My place is here with my people. Why not send Beth Levy? She is making no secret of her desire to replace me in the next election."

Randall offered a shrug. She was holding a small comp-pad in her right hand—an extremely fancy model—and was entering notes with her left. "Your willingness to go to the Baronies and enter direct negotiations will help boost your credibility at the polls."

Arden rolled his eyes.

"The citizens will be glad to see you taking a stronger role. Venturing off world will help increase their confidence. And," she coughed into her hand, "there's also the fact that the Ospma Barons have specifically requested *your* attendance."

"Lucky me."

"Earth ships don't venture beyond the United Human Worlds' borders very often, Prime Minister."

Trudeau looked across the room at the Fleet Admiral. "No, they don't, Arden. The Honourable Member Hidoshi was quite surprised by the request when it arrived."

Arden's expression was vacant as he sipped at his tea.

"Admiral?"

"Sorry..." He gave his head a little shake. "You were saying?"

"We were discussing my trip. Are you lost in thought?"

"Just thinking about the past."

"Anything in particular?"

"Just an old journey beyond the frontier."

* * *

The hatch hissed open and Dale Arden pushed himself through. With the ease born of long practice, his magnetic soled boots clicked securely to the deck even before the hatch had hissed closed behind him. "We're approaching the final transfer point, Admiral. The rest of the task group reports situation normal."

"Excellent news." The admiral had not yet looked up from her desktop. "It has been a long journey."

"Yes, Ma'am." Arden nodded and then reached for the hatch controls.

"Not just yet, Lieutenant." Juanita Fernandez smiled at his confusion. Hints of gray coloured her curly black hair. "This is your first flight beyond the borders of the United Human Worlds?"

"Yes, Ma'am."

"It should prove to be fairly routine, Lieutenant."

"Just pop into the Beta Three system and attempt to open formal trade negotiations with the Goolatch." Arden chuckled weakly. "Yeah, easy."

"The Ospma are our dominant trade partner, but Parliament does not wish that status quo to remain." Fernandez studied the monitor built into her desk. "Information recovered from the recent skirmish at Beta Durani indicates that the Goolatch were once a major power in the galaxy. Their technology is considerably more advanced than Earth's." *Hopefully more advanced than what the pirates were using.*

"So Parliament is hoping that with a trade agreement, we could increase the abilities of UHW Spacey?"

"That is one hope."

"The Ospma won't like it."

"Not our concern."

Arden frowned at her tone. "I am not familiar with other trade agreements." Earth only had dealings with the Ospma. It had been that way since the Ospma first discovered Earth. "Are there any?"

"Not at the moment."

Arden shook his head. "The lack of potential trade partners could have serious repercussions for the United Human Worlds in the long-term."

"We need new technologies. The Ospma keep us on a short leash." Fernandez signed her name on a report and filed it away in her desk.

"The lack of potential trade partners could also mean that the Devastators have already swept around our borders and eliminated everyone else."

"True."

Juanita Fernandez undid her restraints and rose to her feet. "We should head to the bridge then. I don't want to miss our transit back into normal space."

* * *

The bridge was noisy with officers issuing reports.

"Status report?" Juanita Fernandez snapped as she floated through the hatch and onto the bridge.

Dennis McGreggor turned towards her. "All systems are operating normally."

"I should hope so."

"Engineering is confident that the worm-engine will operate correctly." McGreggor wiped his hand through his short beard. "They've been babying the power flow for hours."

"I have every confidence in Chief Lynch." Fernandez moved towards her chair. "If she's made a mistake, after all, we'll all be dead before we know about it."

McGreggor snorted.

Dale Arden took his own seat at the sensor station and secured his restraints. *Here goes the gamble for us all,* he thought. From all appearances, the crew was confident that this would pay-off for them.

McGreggor touched his headset. "Final checks have arrived...all systems are nominal."

"Good. Navigation?"

"We should be in the right place," Sprang replied immediately. "I have a gravity shadow. We've got planets."

"Then you may begin."

Sprang keyed a control, issuing an alert to the entire ship. "All hands, prepare. We're about to commence transit."

"Sound general quarters and then stand by." Fernandez was seated and secured into her command chair. She looked calm and composed as the final seconds ticked past. "Activate the engine!"

McGreggor closed his eyes just long enough to mutter a quick prayer, then nodded.

Sprang reached for a new group of controls only recently added to her console. "Activating now."

The ceiling lights dimmed.

Arden watched his own console. The power drain to the engines was immense. *Everything we've got is going there!*

Fernandez sniffed. "Is something burning?" she asked.

McGreggor shook his head. "My board is still green."

"Wormhole is open!" Sprang called out. "Engine is running hot, but stable. For now," she added.

"Success!"

Fernandez nodded. "This time at least."

Dale Arden licked his lips. The *Odin* had been retrofitted with a worm-engine that had been recovered from a derelict *Warsphere*. *The Ospma have no idea that we have this ship,* he thought. *They won't be happy to learn about its existence either.* The Ospma had been extremely reluctant to allow Humans to build or possess their own worm-engines. *They like to keep us limited and tied to them.*

Fernandez raised her voice. "Commence transit!"

The *Odin* shuddered briefly as it slid through the wormhole back into normal space.

"Transit completed," Sprang announced as the lighting returned to normal conditions. "We're on station, Admiral."

"Scan the system. Communications, begin broadcasting our greeting. All frequencies and channels."

Arden waited for the sensors to complete their scan. *Hopefully the Goolatch can speak Ospma.* He doubted they would know any Human languages—the Humans certainly didn't know how to speak Goolatch. "The rest of the fleet has come through and is in formation. No sign of Goolatch ships in weapon range."

"Continue to scan."

"Aye, Admiral."

"Chief Lynch is checking on the engine now." McGreggor failed to keep the relief from his voice. "So far, he reports no sign of damage."

"Good, once the recharge is complete we should be able to leave again." Fernandez wasn't happy about the long delay in recharge time. "Is it still going to take as long as he thought?"

"Yep." McGreggor nodded. "Five times as long as for the Ospma."

"Damn."

"They *are* the experts at this. I think we're doing good for our first time trying to operate one."

"We will have to remedy that in the future." Fernandez turned her head. "Communications, I'm still waiting."

"Admiral, we are not receiving any signals."

"Impossible." Fernandez shook her head at the negative report. "Beta Three is supposed to be one of their major colonies."

Arden nodded. "As well as being the home base for the Tainba Sector Fleet." *At least according to reports intercepted from messages passing amongst the Ospma Baronies.* "There should be several shipyards present around the third planet."

"*Sleipnir* is not detecting any power emissions from orbit or on the surface." The *Witch of Endor*-class had the most powerful sensor arrays among the TerraGuard Fleet.

"Sprang, are we in the right star system?"

"Navigation confirms our location, Admiral. The database matches the stars. This *is* Beta Three."

She frowned. "Take us in...slow and steady."

Arden checked the displays. The *Odin's* course along the beacons had been simple...Earth to Sirius to Orion to Altair to Epsilon and then across the border into Goolatch space. *We appear to be in Beta Three. Could our information be wrong?* "Could the Ospma have lied to us about the presence of a Goolatch base?"

"It's not their style to lie." Fernandez shook her head as she dismissed the thought. "The Ospma liaisons assigned to Fourth Fleet have always been careful to maintain a powerful garrison on watch in Epsilon. Why waste the effort of keeping their ships if there was no real threat?"

McGreggor snorted. "Who understand the Ospma? Even after all this time?"

"Take us towards the planet, Sprang. Half-speed."

"Yes, Admiral."

The UHW Spacey fleet drifted deeper into the system.

"Full sensor sweeps by all ships," Fernandez ordered. "I don't want anything sneaking up on us."

Arden nodded his head. "Aye, Admiral." He was keeping a careful eye on his displays. "If anything was in range, they'd have seen the wormhole."

"I know, but from all reports the Goolatch are territorial. They should have respond by now." The admiral grimaced. "I hate being surprised."

* * *

Arden straightened in his chair. "Admiral, we have visual contact with the surface."

"Show me." Fernandez turned towards the display.

The planet's surface was barren.

"What did the tactical briefing say about this world?" Fernandez asked in a soft voice. She knew the answer already—everyone present did.

"Most of the planet was tropical, Admiral. Quite pleasant for Humans, if drier than the Ospma themselves prefer." Arden shook his head. The visuals did not match the reports. "Where are the oceans?"

"Beta Three, population estimated at over half a billion." Juanita Fernandez gestured at the display of a barren, dead world. "So what the hell happened here?"

"I don't know." Arden shook his head in shock. "I have no idea."

* * *

"We have confirmed the reports. The last of our shuttles have returned with the surface scouting parties." Arden stiffened to attention, relying on his magnetic-soled shoes to keep him in place. "The surface has been stripped virtually bare."

"Atmospheric readings?" Juanita Fernandez asked.

"Oxygen content is less than ten per cent and continuing to drop. Trace gases are higher than in normal proportions."

"Interesting." McGreggor was also present.

"Scans have failed to detect any significant resource deposits."

"The planet has been strip-mined then?"

"It does appear that way." Juanita studied the comp-pad in her hand. "Anything more to add?"

Arden shook his head sadly. "There are no signs of survivors. If there was a colony here, it's gone without a trace."

"Updates from the rest of the fleet confirm a lack of resources in the system. The asteroid belt has been mined fairly efficiently."

"Admiral, it seems highly unlikely that a reported and known system should be so completely lacking in minerals and other natural resources."

"Oh, it's not unlikely...assuming that the Devastators have passed through." Juanita sighed. "Just like the colony on Kosbrak."

Chapter Nine

Collin Zane lifted his beer stein to his lips. *I've never enjoyed send-offs,* he thought. *Too many times you never see the others again.* The room was crowded with members of his crew and those from other ships preparing for their own missions. *At least I'm in space again.* He could see his *Witch of Endor*-class frigate floating just beyond the reinforced window. It appeared to be moving sedately, but that was just the illusion created by the rotation of the space station.

"Captain Zane?"

With a regretful sigh, Zane turned away from the porthole—no, at this size, it was a window. "Yes, Felix?"

Felix Boxleitner was holding onto the arm of a beautiful, redheaded woman. "This is my wife, Anna."

Zane held out his hand. "A pleasure to meet you."

"And you, Captain." She had a soft voice, a trace of an English accent, and was wearing an expensive and stylish dress. "Felix has been talking about you for weeks now. He's looking forward to shipping out with you."

"I'm certain he will make a fine executive officer." Zane lifted the stein to his lips and took a swallow. "What do you do while he's away on extended missions?"

"I'm an xeno-archeologist."

"She's one of the best," Boxleitner added.

"OPE?"

"Freelancer, actually." She gave him another warm smile.

"Mrs. Boxleitner underrates herself." A slender, dark-haired man approached the gathering. "Her presence is much sought after." He wore a dark suit, cut in the current style.

Anna turned, her cheeks colouring slightly. "Doctor Wasser, you're flattering me."

"Nonsense." He gave them all a disarming smile, showing a row of perfect white teeth. "My colleagues in OPE were very impressed with your work at the Ronspira III ruins. Doctor Sung had nothing but praise for you." Absently, he reached up to stroke the small stone pendent that he wore around his neck.

"More flattery?" Felix asked.

"Off-Planet Explorations want me to join a new expedition." Anna's voice carried a certain degree of eager anticipation. "A six month long-range mission to the rim of known space. The *Marco Polo* is going to investigate the ruins on Alpha Omega."

"The *Marco Polo*?"

"A survey ship," Morden explained. "One of OPE's finest."

"Alpha Omega? I've never heard of that world." Boxleitner looked at his new captain with a shrug. "You?"

After a moment's thought, Zane shook his own head. "New one to me," he admitted, frowning.

"It's off on the rim of known space," Anna explained. "Quite a distance away from any colony or inhabited world."

"It must be," Zane agreed, "if none of us have heard of it."

Wasser gave them a smug smile. "It's quite possibly the planet farthest away from United Human Worlds space that we have yet ventured."

Boxleitner frowned at that. "Anna, I'm not sure I'm comfortable with you going so far away."

"I'll be fine, Felix. Certainly safer than you will be at Beta Durani."

"This seems so sudden."

"*You* get new orders suddenly." Anna laughed at his look of confusion. "Why can't I?"

Zane took a step away. "I should leave you two alone to discuss it." He noticed that Wasser was already engaged in conversation with another man. *Doctor Sung?* He guessed that the Asian man must be Sung. *Could be anyone though.*

"No need for that, Zane. We'll continue this discussion later, Anna."

"Having a lovers' quarrel?"

Zane turned around at that voice. "Kathleen."

Kathleen Levy was smiling. "And here I bet you thought I was going to miss the send-off?" She gave the Boxleitners a warm smile. "Zane tends to keep me hidden away," she told them. "I think he's ashamed to be seen around a Member of Parliament."

"Of course I'm not!"

"You could have fooled me." She held out her hand. "I'm Kathleen Levy."

"Felix Boxleitner. My wife, Anna."

"A pleasure to meet you both. I have hopes that someday Zane will make an honest woman out of me as well."

Zane grunted.

"But I don't see that happening."

"Sometimes having a husband is over-rated," Anna commented.

Felix Boxleitner stood there with his mouth hanging open.

Zane laughed ruefully. "You can't win," he told the other man. "Just let them talk as they will and nod occasionally. Makes them happy."

"And you're the expert?"

"I like to think I've learned a few things."

Levy snorted in a most unladylike fashion.

* * *

Anton Trudeau felt *UHW Spacey One* give a particularly violent shudder and he almost fell out of his chair. "This is one of the reasons why I hate space travel." Another tremble shook the bulkheads. "Are they supposed to creak like that?" He hastily checked his restraints.

"Everything is fine," Arden commented. He was seated comfortably in his chair as the cruiser continued moving through hyperspace.

"Fine you say. I don't even the get dignity of a private space yacht. *UHW Spacey One* is nothing more than a repainted *Deliverance*."

"Then put in a request for a yacht."

"Of course. That *would* do wonders for my approval ratings."

A soft chime sounded.

"*Attention please,*" the captain's voice said over the intercom. "*Fasten your restraints and prepare yourselves. We are about to transit to normal space.*"

"I hate transiting as much as the rest of the travel." Trudeau rechecked his restraints yet again.

Arden chuckled softly. He was quite relaxed. The rather opulent furnishings of the room were more than he was used too, of course, but the Prime Minister could not be seen traveling in a Spartan military warship. *We have appearances to maintain, after all.*

The lights dimmed.

Trudeau gasped.

"It's quite normal," Arden reminded him. "The reactor is shunting extra power to the worm-engines."

"And now we hope that they don't blow up."

"They haven't yet." Arden chuckled again. "You are such a worrier."

The intercom chimed again. "*Wormhole is open and stable...we are now passing through.*"

The modified *Deliverance*-class cruiser shuddered one more time as it opened a wormhole and emerged into normal space.

The cabin lights brightened back towards their normal level.

The intercom chimed again. "*We've entered the Ospma home system, Prime Minister. We are altering course towards the planet. We should enter orbit in approximately six hours.*"

"Thank you, Captain." Trudeau tried to clear his throat. It was too dry. "Hopefully we will not have trouble with our code clearances."

"*I don't anticipate any, Prime Minister. Just sit back and relax.*"

Trudeau grimaced. "It is no great secret that I've never enjoyed space travel, yet even my captain knows it."

"Indeed. And how equally unfortunate that you chose a career requiring such travel." Arden smiled to take the sting from his words. He was leaning back in his own chair, perfectly at ease.

"I had hoped to avoid doing it too often."

Arden grunted sourly. "If the war continues to go badly, you won't have many worlds to visit."

Trudeau looked sharply at his military commander, then frowned. "Hopefully this conference will alter the course of the war then," he said with quiet optimism. "How long before we can see Ospma Prime?"

"Three to four hours most likely. We should have a visual of their wormhole station though."

"It's the same design as *Leonidas* or *Masada*. I don't need to see it." The designs were standardized after all. "The flight here was fairly smooth, I suppose."

"Yes, it was." Arden accepted a drink from a stewardess who had just entered the cabin with a tray. "I've been here before, usually it's a lot more rough."

Trudeau's gray eyebrows lifted. "Rougher?" He waved away the stewardess.

"There are an unusually high number of black holes in the area—a matter the astronomers love to debate. They distort the fabric of space and hyperspace alike. Even the beacons are subject to partial interference."

"Charming."

"It's one of the reasons behind the Ospma's particular propulsion technology."

"And their supposed mastery over hyperspace?"

"Yes, or so we guess." Arden paused to sip at his drink. "I will be interested in seeing who else attends this conference."

"The other powers?"

"How many of them are left?" Arden asked. "The Ospma don't speak much about their neighbours."

Trudeau nodded his agreement. "The various races have stood alone and isolated for too long. They need to be brought together in some kind of interstellar union of worlds."

"Or a league?"

"A League of Independent Races. I should propose such a thing." Trudeau chuckled. "It would be certainly cause a stir."

"I just hope that the Devastators don't hear about this conference. We don't need them to show up."

Trudeau shuddered. "How very true."

* * *

"Approaching worm-point," Michael Jankowski announced from his station. "Thrusters are operating normally."

"We have clearance from *Leonidas*."

Zane nodded his acknowledgement to Boxleitner for his report. "Thank you. Jankowski, open the wormhole."

"Aye, Captain." Signals were hasty transmitted to the station.

Energy crackled around the spine-like projectors mounted along the edges of the ring-shaped *Leonidas*.

The fabric of space was torn open by a wormhole as it swirled into brilliant life. Lightning-like energy bolts crackled around the edges as it stabilized.

Felix Boxleitner swiveled his chair around to face Zane. "Captain, the wormhole is holding itself stable. We're awaiting your orders."

"A dozen terrawatts of energy burned just to allow us to travel to Orion." Zane shook his head at the thought. *More energy expended in one transit than some Earth nations use in a year or more.* "Let's get going. Orion Seven is waiting."

* * *

"We owe you so much, Baron Essan." Anton Trudeau attempted to wave his arms in the appropriate manner of greeting but his best efforts were pre-doomed to failure. *I don't have enough arms to do it right.* He hoped the Ospma would understand his attempt though.

"Payment has been more than adequate." The mauve-coloured Ospma weaved his own arms in a series of complex gestures.

Trudeau grimaced. *I wasn't even close to getting that right*, he thought in bemusement. "You gave us the stars. You saved us."

"Did they?"

Anton Trudeau turned his head towards the rest of his party. "You would disagree, Carnes?" *And in public at that.*

She nodded back at him. "Yes, I do."

Dale Arden grunted. Unlike the civilians in their finest suits and dresses, he was clearly at ease in his uniform. "When the Ospma first contacted us, Humanity was on the verge of another global war. We would have destroyed ourselves."

"The Ospma wanted us to come out into space and fight for them."

"Not at first." Essan's skin mottled and turned a dark plum. "We visited at first without seeking."

"And now we have been given the stars."

"As mercenaries for their war."

Essan shifted so that he could look at Carnes with most of his eyes. "The Devastators would have found your world eventually," he rasped. "How long would you have lasted against them? A primitive species, barely able to reach orbit of its home world?"

"We might not have been found."

"The Devastators hunt relentlessly. Many wormholes twist through the space near Sol...your world guards a valuable nexus." The Ospma's tone was as unreadable as his expression. "We believe that fate would have forced your race into prominence."

Trudeau shook his head. The meeting was being held on an open patio, with open water on three sides of it. The waves looked inviting, for all their murky green appearance, as they crashed against the coral-covered beaches. The air was very hot and very damp and it smelled somewhat musty, but the sun, at least, was warm on his face.

Arden wiped sweat from his forehead. He took a deep breath and coughed.

Trudeau looked at him.

"Something in the air," Arden explained. "But not enough of it," he added. The local atmosphere should be toxic to Humans, but something was keeping the trace gases diluted enough that they could breath. "The humidity will take some getting used too."

"Nine-five per cent I think." Anton Trudeau gestured towards the beach. "The air is shimmering."

Arden frowned. "It's a force field." He barely remembered to keep his voice low. "So that's how they're keeping the patio friendly."

"What do you mean?" Then Trudeau blinked in surprise as he realized exactly where he stood. "Of course...we should be dead from the air."

"Luckily the Ospma want us alive." Arden looked towards their host.

Essan was watching them.

"I have one question," Arden said in a loud voice. "I still want to know where these machines first came from."

"A most excellent question." The speaker who chose that particular moment to step through a door and out onto the patio, was definitely not Ospma. She was humanoid with vaguely feline features—pointed ears and cat's eyes. She was dressed in a black uniform, with medals and ribbons across her jacket breast.

Arden eyed her, then his gaze darted over to one of Trudeau's aides as the blonde woman gave a start. *What is wrong with Miss Winters?* he wondered. "You are another of the Ospma's allies?" he asked the alien.

"We stand alone."

Essan's skin darkened in hue and he undulated across the patio towards her. "You challenge us, Las'li-drac."

She laughed briefly at that, then her tone turned bitter. "Not any more," she replied. "Not for some decades we haven't."

Trudeau turned towards Arden. "Have I missed something?"

Dale Arden's eyes narrowed. "From what I recall from an old briefing, Las'li-drac was once a WarMaster of the Raptchi. They fought minor conflicts against pretty much every other species…until the Devastators came."

She nodded to him. "One of their Gods-damned factory ships found Rachi and attacked it. The planetary surface was stripped bare of every possible resource—raw ore, forests, buildings, people—and then that factory ship constructed a smaller copy of itself and continued to rampage its way through our Imperium."

"You lost your Imperium." Even with his atrocious accent, Essan sounded smug.

"Raptarachi fell," Las'li-drac snarled, "but WarMaster Tor'jon-na made its death count!" Her eyes flashed. "We tied up their fleet, luring them there, and many Silencers were destroyed when Raptarachi Prime went nova. My people there died as heroes."

"A pith that you did not lure *all* of the factory ships to Raptarachi then." Essan's tone was heavy with amusement. "At least one survived."

Her yellow eyes flashed. "There was peace for a long time."

"But the Devastators returned."

"Yes." Las'li-drac licked her lips. "So far our remaining Imperium has been ignored by the Silencers."

"The same cannot be said for our worlds," Trudeau commented. "We have lost thirty colonies in the last fifty years."

"We have all lost worlds to these machines." The new speaker looked vaguely Human, but his nose was more pointed and his canine teeth were more elongated than the Human norm. His skin was hidden beneath thick, curly fur, with his hair styled into a high crest. He was followed by another alien, who had similar features though his crest was shorter.

"Ambassador Dajo."

"Essan." He nodded, then gestured to the man at his side. "My aide, Morla Larmo." He waited a moment before continuing. "Essan, I see that you *did* mean to invite *everyone* to this little conference of yours. The Raptchi." He nodded coolly to Las'li-drac. "Your pet Humans, of course, were definitely expected."

Essan waved his tentacle-arms. "The Goolatch are certainly welcome."

"Of course we are welcome. Our mighty Republic has spread itself across hundreds of worlds, bringing them the wonders and advancements of our modest civilization."

Trudeau blinked at Dajo's grand tone. His own dark coloured suit was downright somber compared to the sartorial splendor of the Goolatch's rich clothing. *More gold trim than a brigade of admirals back home. He looks like some Napoleonic officer.*

Arden was also studying the various arrivals.

"Before you get too excited by my presence, you should be made aware that the Goolatch will not be committing the bulk of our fleets to any Ospma-dominated United Human Worlds. Let it be understood that we Goolatch expect to hold a key place in any offensive."

Las'li-drac grimaced. "The Raptchi Imperium will not place its military *pentacons* under *Goolatch* commanders."

"Then we are at an impasse, yes?" Dajo held out his hands in a placating gesture. "And the Devastators will destroy us all."

Essan coiled his limbs around his body.

Trudeau sighed. "This may take some work," he muttered to Arden.

"You're the politician."

"I know, I know."

· Chapter Ten

Anton Trudeau sniffed at the drink in his hand. *I've smelled worse things,* he reminded himself. "The conference continues at least. No one has gone home yet."

"Talking is easy...a pity we could not convince the Devastators to sit down and talk." Dajo was holding an ornately decorated goblet in his hand. "At least a machine would be more rational than the other delegates."

"The Ospma or the Raptchi?"

"Either. Both." Dajo smiled and then took a long swallow of the drink. "Drink up, Prime Minister, this is a fine vintage. One of the best in recent years."

Trudeau took a sip. The liqueur was fruity and sour on his tongue, with a spicy aftertaste. "This isn't half bad."

Dajo chuckled as he refilled his goblet. "You Earthers are an interesting species. Not at all what I expected from the reports delivered by our spies."

Trudeau chose to ignore the comment about spies. "What did you expect?"

"You are supposed to be primitives used as simple soldiers for your Ospma masters." He laughed again. "With a slight twist of fate, you would have been the masters of the galaxy as we once were. Great Maker, you could even have been *Goolatch.*"

"We don't want to rule the galaxy." Trudeau shook his head. "We just want peace."

"Peace? What is peace? The galaxy is a place of turmoil. Constant chaos and conflict. If not the Devastators, then it would be someone else. The Raptchi perhaps."

"Then you see no hope?"

"Hope? Of what value is hope?" Dajo laughed a third time and took another drink. "I trust my weapons and my fellow Goolatch. Beyond that, nothing."

"Then why come to the conference?"

"The Devastators are very powerful and dangerous. We must defeat them if we are to survive as a species. If *any* species is too survive. We have talked and debated amongst ourselves and so the Goolatch are represented in this grand conference." He took a drink. "Perhaps nothing will come of it, save talk, and perhaps we will figure out a path to victory."

"Do you have hope?"

"Without hope, there is no point in living." Dajo smiled, baring his teeth. "Well, there is a point in having this fine *varishy* to drink."

Trudeau smiled. "Wine, women, and song?"

"A fine saying your people have." Dajo refilled their glasses. "As you say, 'wine, women, and song'!"

* * *

"Scanning the area now," Christoph Wolfgang announced from his station.

Collin Zane adjusted the straps holding him into his chair. The bridge of his *Hellstorm* was calm and businesslike. *The way it should be.* His mouth twitched into a smile. *It usually isn't, but it's the way a starship should be run.* "Find anything, Wolfgang?"

"Beta Durani is still broadcasting. There're a lot of signals were being transmitted, but not what we're watching for." He switched between comm frequencies even as he gave his report.

"Scan for distress signals."

"Yes, Sir." His tone bordered on annoyance. "Nothing yet."

"Well, Exec?"

Boxleitner shrugged in his chair. "I don't know what to say, Captain. The Devastators are almost certainly in the system, but we should have had some contact with them by now."

"I'm sure we'll find them soon enough."

"And then the fun can begin?"

"Don't worry, you wanted action and you're going to get all you can handle. We'll charge in with all guns blazing."

"I'm glad to hear that," Boxleitner replied with a grin. "I was afraid I might get bored."

Wolfgang turned his head. "Captain, I'm picking up a distress signal!"

"Course and bearing?"

"Downloading it to the helm now." Wolfgang paused. "It's a Devastator patrol carrier."

"Wonderful." Zane grimaced. "The universe wouldn't want us to get too bored now, would it?"

"Should we alter course?"

"We have no choice, Commander Boxleitner." Zane looked away from his exec. "Jankowski, do it."

"Intercept course plotted," Michael Jankowski announced in a confident voice. "Accelerating to full speed."

"ETA?"

"Twenty minutes."

"Commander Boxleitner, sound battle stations."

"Aye, Captain." Felix reached for the controls. "This is definitely where the fun begins."

* * *

The door to the office was closed and the windows were curtained. *Overall, the room is decorated with suitable taste and style for a Human. I can't see an Ospma being happy staying here though.* Even the air was less humid than normal for the planet. *They are making every effort then.* Trudeau turned to his aide. "Well?"

Tabitha Winters offered a shrug. "They are *alien*," she explained. "I can't read their thoughts clearly."

"But you *can* sense something?"

"A bit...but it's cold and...well, alien."

"Keep trying."

"I will." Her hand brushed the lapel of her dark green jacket, as if searching for a broach. "It just feels...*wrong*."

"The United Human Worlds needs every advantage we can get, Miss Winters. Do whatever you can to alleviate these feelings, but scan them at every opportunity. We have to know what they're thinking."

"Yes, Prime Minister."

Trudeau turned away from her to look at another member of his diplomatic party. "What word from Earth?"

"Nothing much." Arden shrugged. "Patrols have been dispatched, but overall, there's no sign of Devastator activity. The United Human Worlds are currently at peace."

"Peace is relative."

"I know that." Arden leaned back in the chair, listening to the springs creak. "The war is not over. I know the Devastators will strike sooner or later."

"They always do."

"The Devastators are the greatest threat in the galaxy."

"Another reason for making this conference successful. We need strong allies."

"Other than the Ospma."

"Yes, other than the Ospma."

* * *

Zane leaned forward in his chair. "Wolfgang, identify the targets."

"One carrier...a dozen drones so far."

"What's their target?"

"They're attacking an ore refinery. Its defences are down." Not that it very likely ever had much in the way of defensive weaponry to start with. "The crew are already abandoning it."

"Accelerate us to attack speed. Cover the life pods as they run."

Boxleitner's eyes scanned his own displays. "The carrier has spotted us, Captain. It's coming about...additional drones launching."

"Charge the surge cannons."

"The other drones have broken off their attack runs on the refinery."

Twenty-four drones were closing quickly.

"Of course, we're the better target."

"Aren't you glad that you transferred onboard, Felix?" Zane chuckled. "Your first voyage is going to be a fun one."

"I've survived worse than this, Captain."

"Good." Zane called up a visual onto the display built into the arm of his chair as the drones closed with his ship. They were the same design as every other one on record: a ball-shaped fuselage, with rectangular solar panel wings, powered by blue-glowing twin ion engines. "All batteries, fire at will."

The drones dodged with maneuvers too sharp and violent for piloted craft to survive. Twelve fighters closed with the *Hellstorm*; seven survived long enough to rake the cruiser's hull with greenish laser light.

"Minimal damage. Hull armour holding." The drones were like mosquitoes...a lot of small bites to take down their prey. "The second wave is closing now."

"All gunners, open fire!" Gerald Kemp ordered.

Surge cannons continued firing and three more drones exploded.

"At least they die easily." Felix was watching the screens closely.

"Find me that carrier!" Zane kept his voice steady. "Load the missile tubes."

"Carrier sighted."

The blocky ship was hovering near the equally blocky refinery. Green flashes marked the carrier's efforts to destroy life pods as they launched from the refinery.

"Give them a volley!" At Zane's order, the *Hellstorm's* surge cannons fired and bolts of energy skittered across the normally invisible ray shielding and raked the carrier's dark hull. Explosions blossomed as several of the bolts struck home to short out and overload the electronics. "Continue firing."

"Their shields are disrupted!"

"Fire the missiles!"

Kemp nodded. "Giving it cover fire!" The surge cannons fired again.

The missiles slipped past the handful of drones still flying, and impacted on the carrier's hull in a flash of nuclear energy.

"Direct hit." Boxleitner looked away from his display as another bright flash lit the screen. "Its shields are gone!"

"Kemp!"

"Firing!" Kemp activated the frigate's main gun—the electro-magnetic bolter fired a powerful blast of raw energy channeled straight from the quantum singularity. "Carrier destroyed."

"They're tough foes, despite being automated, but I have yet to see a ship that can survive having a nuclear warhead detonate against their engine bank." Zane smiled and leaned back in his chair. "Clear up the last of those drones," he ordered, "and then proceed to recover the life pods." He kept his voice calm. *That was too easy,* he thought grimly. *Where are the big boys?*

* * *

"Why don't we see more Goolatch?" Arden asked Larmo in a soft tone of voice. The enclosed balcony overlooked a small rocky beach. Waves splashed against the brightly coloured coral and the black rocks. "You were rumoured to control a large swathe of territory. Large enough to worry the Ospma. So why haven't we encountered you more often?"

Larmo shrugged. "Because you inhabit a dull and uninteresting portion of the galaxy and we see little cause to visit you?" Then, abruptly he threw his head back and laughed.

Arden frowned. *Their sense of humour takes some getting used too,* he thought to himself.

Larmo sobered. "You sent ships to Beta Three," he said.

Arden nodded. "Decades ago."

"You saw our great colony there, yes?"

"I saw a dead world."

Larmo's eyes narrowed at the Earther's dull tone.

"We had read reports about Beta Three, and when we arrived we found only a dead world. An entire star system stripped of every useful resource."

"Beta Three fell to a massive Devastator assault. The Tainba Sector Fleet fought with gallantry and skill and eventually with suicidal desperation." Larmo gave a rather Human-sounding sigh. "We lost Beta Three. And we lost Torco. We even lost Tainba. The mighty Goolatch Republic was whittled away world by world...but at the end, we *held* and destroyed a Devastator fleet at Ashgor. We still have the hulk of a factory ship drifting in orbit as a monument to the billions of lives lost."

Arden listened to the bitterness in Larmo's voice as a fresh series of waves crashed against the rocks below. "I'm sorry."

"It is, as you have said, a grim fact. You Earthers have lost numerous colonies as well—thirty in the last fifty years, yes?"

"Yes."

"My people once ruled more than three hundred worlds. We have barely a quarter of them still proudly Goolatch. The Ospma have only a few holdings to their name, not counting your own worlds. The Raptchi have lost most of their own imperium, despite their current delusions of greatness." He spread his arms. "And so it goes. The

Devastators rampage across our galaxy and we can do little to stop them."

"We are not giving up, Ambassador." Arden shook his head. "Humans do not surrender."

"Ah, neither do Goolatch."

"That could prove to be a useful piece of common ground."

"Yes, it could at that." Larmo nodded. "It could indeed."

Chapter Eleven

"You saw the defenses around Ospma Prime?"

"And took detailed sensor readings, Prime Minister." Dale Arden paced slowly along the corridors of Altair IV Transfer Station, following just behind Anton Trudeau. "Three of their ring bases and scores of *Starsphere* OWPs. A formidable defensive barrier. I didn't get a final count on the number of warships present at the time." No doubt the number of ships varied as ships were dispatched on missions and new hulls were built. *How many ships would they rally to the final defence of their home world?* he wondered. *How many* can *they have left?*

"No firm military numbers, aside from what they report."

"I do not believe our allies have ever told us the full truth about their military strength."

"Any more than we have." Trudeau knew that the Joint Chiefs routinely understated UHW Spacey's strength in reports as a precaution.

"We don't believe that the Devastators can tap into our databanks when they consume a ship, station, or world, but why take a chance?"

"I have never spoken against that policy."

"It's an unspoken policy at best."

Trudeau nodded at two technicians as he walked past them. "So," he continued after they were out of earshot, "from what you have seen, are the Baronies' defenses sufficient to hold Ospma Prime?"

"I doubt it." Arden shook his head. "No defense seems to hold back the Devastators when they come in force."

Marc Gascoigne fell into step with them. "And you still feel that the conference was less than successful?"

"It was a successful meeting of likeminded delegates," Arden told the commander of the Fourth Fleet. "The press releases will do some good for morale."

"But?" Trudeau prompted.

"We have promises to share data and coordinate some military actions and efforts...but whether anything solid will actually come from the talks, I cannot say."

"The Prime Minister's speech—"

"Trudeau was talking to his fellow politicians and the civilians. He put a pleasant spin on the conference, but overall I would not expect to see large numbers of alien warships suddenly appearing at our colonies."

"I see." Gascoigne chewed at his lip. "The war will proceed as it has been going then."

"Indeed." Arden forced a smile onto his face. "But then I am a soldier, not a politician, and it is certainly possible that the Prime Minister did indeed obtain some valuable agreements from the delegates."

"I learned not to drink more than two glasses of *varishny*."

Still laughing, the two officers stepped into a lounge. The domed ceiling was open to a view of space.

Trudeau sighed. The sight was nice.

"Fourth Fleet remains at full strength, Prime Minister. We could divert a few additional squadrons to reinforce Sixth Fleet."

"I will take that offer under advisement."

Arden said nothing.

"It won't be enough will it?"

"Kapteyn will hold." Arden forced his words to sound confident. *It has too. This isn't first contact at Kosbrak...*

* * *

"We're now approaching the unidentified object." Alan Chafin kept his voice calm and steady as he verified the sensor readings on his console.

"Increase power to the sensor array." Oscar Jankowski adjusted one of his seat restraints—it was pressing on his leg and would likely leave a bruise later. "Any response to our hails?"

"Nothing yet, Captain."

"Take us in closer."

Several of the bridge crew exchanged nervous looks.

"Aye, Captain," the helmsman finally said.

The cruiser trembled as it accelerated ponderously.

"Full power to the sensors. I want to know everything you can tell me." He was staring at the screen.

"Scanning now..still can't determine much detail."

"Any match in the warbook?"

"Nothing in our records. No match in the Ospma database either."

"It's an alien ship," Jankowski muttered. "First contact." His name would go down in the history books for sure. *Oscar Jankowski, born Prague, Earth, United Human Worlds, was captain of the* Quetzalcoatl, *assigned to UHW Spacey's Fifth Fleet. While on routine patrol of the only recently colonized Kosbrak system, he discovered a vessel from a previously unknown alien species.*

"It appears to be a ship." Alan Chafin checked the display on his console again. Its light reflected dimly from his face. "It's a big one."

"Show it to us." The visual which appeared on the main display was somewhat blurry. "Magnify it."

"Working on it." Chafin nodded his head.

The ship appeared to be huge. Tall and blocky, like a pair of space-going apartment complexes joined together by a shorter one laying on its side.

Oscar Jankowski was smiling in contentment. "It's completely alien." He could heard the eagerness in his voice. "And it's all ours."

Chafin shook his head. "Silhouette still doesn't match anything in the database. Nothing like this has been recorded before."

"Anything else from the sensors?"

"We're still scanning it, Captain. Minimal power emissions...I think it's been abandoned."

"Download all information and relay our sensor scans back to the colony. Have the administrator contact our allies. Maybe the Ospma will recognize it." His smile was growing wider as he saw his fame growing. *That* Encyclopedia Terranica *entry is getting longer and more detailed!*

"I doubt it, Sir. If they knew it was here, they would have salvaged it by now." Kosbrak was on the edge of the Baronies.

"But Kosbrak is recognized as United Human Worlds territory. We found the derelict first, so we get to salvage it."

"Could be a rich prize, eh Captain?"

"You said it, Chafin." Jankowski smiled happily. "Salvaging that derelict could advance Earth technology a thousand years." *Far more valuable to us than anything we've salvaged so far from that dead civilization down on Kosbrak.*

"And give us an advantage over the Ospma?"

"That as well." It was an unspoken wish throughout UHW Spacey that discoveries would be made which would allow Humanity to decrease its reliance on the Ospma Baronies. "Scramble a flight of shuttles and send them in for a closer look. See if they can spot any airlocks or hanger bays."

"Aye, Captain."

"If not, we'll just have to burn our way onboard." His entry in the *Encyclopedia Terranica* was definitely growing longer. *Oscar Jankowski, born Prague, Earth, United Human Worlds, was captain of the* Quetzalcoatl, *assigned to UHW Spacey's Fifth Fleet. While on routine patrol of the only recently colonized Kosbrak system, he discovered a vessel from a previously unknown alien species. Though a major discovery at the time, Jankowski's true claim to fame came when he led a fleet of advanced warships to....*

"I have the latest scan results for you, Captain."

Looking across the *Quetzalcoatl's* bridge, Jankowski accepted the comp-pad from his exec. "Are these readings accurate?" he demanded after he read the small screen.

"Yes, Captain." Chafin was floating weightlessly in the air, above the deck. "We estimate the object measures over five thousand metres in length and half that much in height."

"Five kilometres in length." The UHW Spacey captain shook his head in disbelief at the sheer scale of it. "No ship can possibly be *that* large." It dwarfed most space stations!

"Those are the readings we have, Sir."

"And it *is* a ship?"

"Apparently." Chafin reached over to tap a button on the pad. "Those appear to be engines. Given the radiation scoring, we guess it to be an ionic drive."

"So it can move under its own power." *Ionic drives were exceedingly rare from what the Ospma tell us.*

"We have no way of knowing how quickly though. They might just be station-keeping thrusters."

"No, I don't think that they are. It's a ship...otherwise it would orbitting a planet or something."

"It might have drifted out of orbit...."

"No, it's a ship." Jankowski was certain of it. "And it's not from Kosbrak?"

"The surface technology and hull alloys don't match anything found down on Kosbrak. I don't think the natives had space travel when they died out."

"No matter." The captain was still grinning as he stared at the displays. *It's mine! All mine.*

"The shuttles are continuing to make scanning runs, but so far they haven't found any obvious docking bays."

"There must be some."

"It's an alien ship. We might not recognize a docking bay as such. The docking bay hatches are probably sealed tight."

"Then arrange to blast a way in."

"That would risk damage—"

Jankowski stared through the small viewport at the vast hulk. "I think the derelict is large enough to handle have a few holes being blown into it."

"Yes, Sir."

Jankowski turned back to a current display. "I don't particularly want to go blasting holes in it either. Be really awful if we blew up their main engines or something we could use ourselves."

"Aye, Sir."

"Still, it's a big ship. The odds are we'll just blow open a hole into a corridor or cargo bay."

"We'll do our best."

"I suspect we should try to go in from the top. The bridge could be there." Jankowski took a deep breath. "Have a team prepped to go aboard. I'm more than halfways tempted to join them."

Green light flashed brighly against the dark hulk.

"What was that?"

"Replay the visual," Jankowski ordered as the rest of the bridge crew gave their full attention to their instruments.

Chafin hurriedly flung himself back to his console. "Energy spike...some kind of energy weapon. Shuttle two destroyed!"

"Damn it! What's happening out there?"

"Reading additional energy spikes. We're being scanned."

"Recall the remaining shuttles," Jankowski ordered. "Sound battle stations."

Chafin hastily buckled his restraints. "Energy spike...massive energy readings from within the object."

"How massive?"

"It's off the scale."

Jankowski shook his head in disbelief. "No...you said it was a derelict."

"The object is moving."

"Projected course?"

"Kosbrak."

Jankowski turned. "Kosbrak?" he repeated.

"Estimating arrival in...ten hours at current speed. If it accelerates, it could be there a lot faster."

I know that. "We have nearly twenty thousand colonists down there. My *family* is down there"

"*Juitzilopochtli* and *Chalchiuhtlicue* are moving to assume flanking positions."

"We are ready to recover shuttles."

"My grandson, Michael is down on that colony. We can't allow that ship to get any closer." Jankowski grunted. "*Quetzalcoatl* to all ships, open fire!"

"Captain?"

"You heard me, Chafin. I said 'open fire.'" His voice was harsh. "They have made no response to our hails, no attempts at communicating, and they just open fire on our shuttles. All ships, return fire!"

"Firing lasers."

Jankowski cursed softly.

"Minimal effect!" Chafin reported a moment later.

"What?"

"Minimal damage to target."

"You missed? Something that size and you *missed*?"

"We hit it, but it's got some kind of force field protecting it."

"Keep firing!" Jankowski grimaced as he realized the second laser volley was as ineffectual as the first.

"Energy spike!"

The *Quetzalcoatl* shuddered as bolts of green energy slammed into its hull.

"Multiple impacts across our ventral hull!" Justin Sisler called out over the sudden wail of alarms. "We've got depressurization!"

Hull breeches. Jankowski cursed loudly. *Every spacers' worst nightmare.* "Load all missile bays! Maybe they'll do something."

"Going evasive," the helmsman called out.

The missiles launched.

"Flying on course...impact now!"

Armour plating shattered in fiery explosions.

"Yes!"

Jankowski frowned. "Chafin, what the hell happened to their shields?"

"I don't know. They don't seem to stop missiles."

"Only our lasers?"

"Yes, Captain."

"Interesting." *The techies will have a field day with this.* "Reload missile bays and continue firing."

A flurry of green energy bolts raked the *Juitzilopochtli*.

The *Chalchiuhtlicue* returned fire with its own batteries.

"The ship is still heading towards Kasbrak."

"*Still?*"

"Aye, Captain."

"We hit with a spread of nukes."

"I know, Sir, but it's a pretty big target."

"Continue to fire all batteries. We have to disable it."

"This is going to make one hell of a log entry," Chafin grunted as the *Quetzalcoatl* groaned under full acceleration.

So much for my history entry.... Jankowski closed his eyes. *Oscar Jankowski, born Prague, Earth, United Human Worlds, was captain of the* Quetzalcoatl, *assigned to UHW Spacey's Fifth Fleet. While on routine patrol of the only recently colonized Kosbrak system, he discovered a vessel from a previously unknown alien species. Though a major discovery at the time, Jankowski's was killed aboard his ship when the derelict attacked Kosbrak.*

Chapter Twelve

"I trust that the *Eye of Ra* meets with your approval, Admiral?"

Dale Arden nodded his head as he surveyed the *Deliverance's* bridge. "So far it does. You run a tight ship, Captain Chapman."

Marcus Chapman stood more straight. He clasped his hands behind his back. "I do my duty for UHW Spacey."

"That's all we can ask." Arden winced at the platitude even as he mouthed the words. *So inadequate*, he thought.

"Admiral Singh seemed interested in our mission."

"That doesn't surprise me in the slightest."

"Admiral Jarrell has also requested a copy of any data gained from the exercises."

Arden nodded again. "I'm not surprised by that either." A short bark of laughter escaped him. "That only thing that *does* surprise me is that neither of them have shown up here to oversee these exercises in person."

David Corwin chose that moment to approach them, carrying a comp-pad in his right hand.

Chapman chuckled. "Admirals Singh and Jarrell were planning to attend, but they were called away at the last minute."

"Where?"

"The Wolf Shipyards I believe."

Arden looked at Corwin with a frown. "Strange that I was not notified of any meeting taking place there." He gave his head a shake. "Sabrina is hosting a meeting?"

"I believe the meeting was actually Singh's idea."

"This is hardly the time for political infighting," Marcus Chapman argued. "We are facing the greatest crisis in human history."

"We have been fighting the Devastators for centuries," Arden replied with tired resignation in his voice. "Since the fall of Kosbrak. I do not see that changing any time soon."

"Perhaps."

"I was present fifty-three years ago when the *Odin* transited into Tainba and found the expected Centuari colony to simply be gone. I was first officer onboard the *Yen-Lo-Wang* when Second Fleet covered the desperate retreat from Avalon to Jericho." He shook off the bitter and painful memories. "Captain Chapman, I believe that we are late for the exercise."

"I believe you are correct, Admiral." Chapman turned to an aide. "Ship's status?"

"All systems are fully operational, Captain. The *Eye of Ra* is ready to begin."

"And our allies?"

"The rest of the battlegroup is holding on station."

"Good."

"Incoming comm signal."

Chapman turned his head. "Let's hear it, Mister Ortega."

Static hissed from the comm-system. "*Test ready?*"

"Yes, it is, Gasak." Chapman offered a smile to Arden. "We are ready to engage in the battle simulation with your *Warsphere*."

"*Good.*" The Ospma sounded pleased. "*Powering up now.*"

"Battle stations!" Chapman's voice cut across the *Eye of Ra's* bridge. "Power to weapons, stand by to engage."

Arden watched without commenting. He knew that the weapons were powered down—they would register hits, but not cause any actual damage to the Ospma's hulls. *Nor will their weaponry damage us.*

"Captain?"

Chapman turned his head. "Yes?"

"Yes, Juegan?"

The sensor officer took a deep breath before he spoke up. "We have a reported energy spike. Attempting to get a sensor lock now."

Chapman took a breath of his own. "Wormhole?"

"Yes, I think so."

"Not at the standard points?"

"No, Admiral, it avoided the transit stations. This is the rough location." The area on the display still covered millions of square kilometres. "I'm trying to tighten the sensor readings."

Arden keyed for the comm. "Is that an Ospma ship arriving, Gasak?"

"None of my people would come that way."

Arden accepted that fact. *Opening a wormhole was fairly easy compared to directing one...getting one to open deep within a star system's gravity was a magnitude more complicated than using a low-gravity point.* "Juegan, try to pinpoint it."

"Aye, Sir."

"Gasak, can you get a better lock."

"No. We must investigate this intruder and destroy them immediately."

Arden frowned. *That seems like a rather harsh decision. They might be friendly.* "I'll take your advice under advisement, Gasak."

Chapman was staring at him now. "Do you think it's the Devastators?"

"Who else?" Arden replied. "Break up the battle group and dispatch scouts to that area. Transmit a system-wide warning. My authourity."

"Aye, Sir."

Chapman grimaced. "So much for the simulation."

"Now the exercise will be so much more interesting."

* * *

"Captain!"

Chapman pushed himself away from the tactical station. "Yes, Juegin?"

"What do you have?" Arden kept his voice crisp as he made his own way to the sensor station. Hours of waiting had worn at him and endless mugs of tea had done little to improve matters.

Juegin looked tired, but he had refused to take a break from his station. "We have a sensor lock on the intruder."

"Where?"

"Very close actually. We're almost within visual range."

"Have you alerted UHW Spacey?" Arden demanded.

"Yes, but with just a general message of a unexpected wormhole opening. No sense in causing a panic until there was actually something definite to report."

"I suppose." *This could just be a false alarm,* Arden thought. *Please let it be a false alarm.*

Marcus Chapman was still talking. "Ortega will broadcast a full alert once we know what we're actually facing."

"Hopefully we're not facing a full invasion fleet." That was Arden's greatest nightmare. *And everyone else's as well.* "Are the weapon systems ready?"

Chapman nodded. "All systems are now at full power." The *Eye of Ra's* weaponry had been powered down to minimal levels for the planned combat simulation. "We're at full output."

"Good."

"Contact!" Juegan called out. "Hard lock on intruder...Captain, the ship is *not* a Devastator design. Power emissions are not consistent with Devastator norms either."

"Visual!" Chapman called out. "Show me what you've got."

"It's a Raptchi ship." Arden frowned as tactical data scrolled across the monitor. "That's a Raptchi dreadnaught."

"Who are the Raptchi?"

"Another race fighting the Devastators," Arden explained. He was very surprised to see that ship. "Corwin will forward you a full report later."

Frowning, Captain Chapman nodded. "So these are new allies then?"

"Maybe." Arden was frowning. *But why come here now?*

"What would the Raptchi be doing here?"

"I'm not sure. Ortega, open a comm-channel."

* * *

The heavy hatchway hissed closed with a distinctive *clunk* as it sealed.

"I didn't believe that the Raptchi Navy had any dreadnaughts left." Dale Arden managed to speak the words without his accent mangling them too badly. "From what reports I've seen, your fleet was supposedly decimated." The room was fairly spartan, with just a handful of chairs, a solid-looking desk, and a few cabinets. *Not very ornate for the captain's quarters,* he thought.

"The Ospma don't know as much as they claim." Las'li-drac shrugged as she offered him a tooth-hidden smile from her chair. "Some few survived the final battle of Raptarachi. The Imperium has been rebuilding its fleet. That's been a high level priority of ours." She rose to her feet in a smooth, cat-like manner and paced across her quarters to a small cabinet. She removed a bottle, uncorked it, and then poured out two glasses. "A taste of *driskata*, Admiral?" Las'li-drac offered a glass of the pale green liquid to Arden. "The Ospma have assured me that this alcohol is biologically compatible with your species."

"Unless that is one of things they were lying about?" he countered. He adjusted his gun holster so that it was not digging into his hip.

She smiled at him again.

"No risk, no glory." Arden accepted a glass and sniffed at the bitter liquid. "Why did you request this meeting, Las'li-drac? Why fly all the way to the Sol System?"

"No risk, no glory."

He stared back at her, unsmiling. *How did she learn Earth's location?* he wondered. *Did the Ospma tell her?*

She took a sip of her drink. "I came because I thought that you would be interested in learning more secrets about the *Silencers*."

"The Ospma have given us countless briefings."

"No doubt." She was still smiling. "But do they truly know *everything* that they claim too?" She took a long drink from her glass. "We Raptchi have been star-faring for just as long, if not longer. We have explored considerably more territory than the Ospma Baronies lay claim too. We have had dealings with many sentient species." Her mouth twitched. "We have heard a great many things."

"Such as?"

"The Silencers emerged from the void beyond the Rim nearly five centuries ago. One massive factory ship appeared, drifting through barren space with just the most minimal power emissions to betray its presence. Its hull was battered and broken with the scars of past battles. It was found by scouts from a race known as the Stellar Association who attempted to board it. Their attempts awakened the Derelict's computer...and the reactivated factory ship consumed the scouts.

"From that one incident, the Silencer threat began. The factory ship found the Stellar Association and consumed their worlds, stripping them one-by-one of every possible resource and then using those raw materials to build copies of itself as well as carriers and drone-fighter craft."

"How do you know this?" Arden raised his own glass and chuckled. "It makes for a fine story, but no one knows where these ships came from."

"They came from beyond the Rim. From the handful of star charts we examined, it looks like they were constructed in another galaxy."

"As I said, it makes for a truly fine story, Las'li-drac, but where is your proof?"

"We captured a factory ship."

Arden froze, the glass almost to his lips. "Impossible."

"No, merely *difficult*. The cost in destroyed warships was immense, but we were able to cripple and board one."

Arden shook his head in disbelief.

"Where did you think we had obtained the technology to generate this artificial gravity?" she asked him. "You don't see sections of *my* ship spinning."

He shrugged. "I had wondered about that when I stepped off my shuttle. What other advanced technology do you have?"

"All in good time. A refill?"

"No, thank you."

Las'li-drac settled back into her chair. "The Silencers are mobile factories...each one is a huge, completely automated structure with technologies far beyond anything we have developed. Certainly far beyond the Ospma and Goolatch as well."

"An fully-automated factory?"

"Named *Silencer-Four* according to the databanks we decoded."

Arden nodded. *So that's why you call them* Silencers *and not* Devastators. "How could you decode what must have been a truly alien database?"

"Decades of work. By ourselves...and by our slaves."

"Slaves? The Ospma never said that you—"

"The Ospma were not worth the effort to conquer. The Raptchi are not a lesser species, Human," her voice had deepened into a growl. "We overcame threats to our existence since long before we achieved spaceflight. The galaxy just offers more threats towards our survival which we must overcome. We have met other races and took whatever steps were necessary to ensure our survival." Her voice thawed slightly. "A lesson you might also want to learn."

Arden shook his head.

"The Silencers came to the Imperium in strength and our fleet was spent like buckets of water thrown into a raging forest fire. Minor successes in one battle, but always another threat erupting elsewhere."

"If you have all this captured data, then why not tell us at the conference?"

"No one was interested. You heard the other delegates...like children in a playground. The Ospma don't trust bipeds—and they only use your people to further their own ambitions. The Goolatch want to be the rulers over everyone else. The handful of other intelligent species prefer to hide and pray to their non-existent gods that the Silencers do not discover them."

"If the Goolatch desire a rebirth of their imperial domains, then what about the Raptchi? Do you want to expand your empire?"

"Not anymore...now we only desire survival."

"A fine story."

"It is a simple truth. We no longer have the battle fleets to try and conquer the galaxy. Our Imperium has been reduced to a fraction of its former size and strength." She lowered her voice, narrowing her eyes. "Just as your own United Human Worlds grows ever weaker and weaker. How long before the Ospma abandon you for some other race of would-be champions?"

"We are their allies, not their slaves."

"So you believe."

"What do you want, Las'li-drac?"

Her mouth twisted into a smile. "Survival. So should you, Dale Arden. So should you."

Something buzzed.

"Yes?" Las'li-drac called.

"The Earther's ship is continuing to hail him. They are growing alarmed at his lack of response to their hails."

"Remove the jamming then." She looked at Arden with a polite smile. "Precautions."

"Of course," he replied in a neutral tone. His comm-link buzzed. "Arden here," he spoke into the mic.

"*Admiral, are you all right?*"

"Of course, Captain Chapman."

"*We've been trying to contact you for some time without success. We think you were being jammed.*"

"A security precaution by WarMaster Las'li-drac. It has since been cancelled. What is your status?"

"*We have received another urgent signal from the Prime Minister.*" Chapman's voice was scratchy with static. "*He demands to know what is happening out here.*"

"Inform him that there is no evidence of Devastator activity in the Sol System."

"As yet," Las'li-drac commented softly.

Arden shot a glance towards her. "Do not mention that the intruder is a Raptchi vessel either."

"*What should I tell him?*"

"Natural phenomena. I don't want the Raptchi's presence being broadcast around the system. The Ospma might take offense."

Las'li-drac was smiling. "Yes, I do believe they might."

"We'll have to try and keep Gasak away from here as well. Stand by, Captain. I'll be back shortly. Out." Arden deactivated his com-link and clipped it back onto his belt.

"If the Silencers come in force, you will be unable to stop them."

"Seeing as you are unwilling to trade us weapons' technology?" He paused for a moment. "We cannot allow our home world to fall...anymore than you could abandon Raptarachi."

"Perhaps." Las'li-drac smiled. "But we knew that our star was unstable and would soon destroy itself. Baiting a trap to lure the Silencers to their destruction was too important a chance to pass up."

"Sol is stable. There is no risk of a nova."

"A pity." The Raptchi WarMaster laughed at his startled expression.

Arden finished his drink, nearly coughing on the harshness of the alcohol. "Share your technology with us."

"Why?"

"We could do great things with it. We could destroy the Devastators and save all of our worlds."

"And then be wiped out in some great war? No, the War Council does not wish to share the Silencer's technology at this time."

"You are dooming potential allies."

"Perhaps." She shrugged. "I wished to take the measure of your in your home ground."

"And?"

She paused.

"Did I pass your test then?"

Las'li-drac continued to smile. "Have a safe flight home, Admiral."

"And to you as well," he replied.

Chapter Thirteen

"Cap?"

"Yes, Boyd?"

"I'm picking up energy emissions at the edge of sensor range."

Durie frowned. "A patrol, ye reckon?"

"I don't think so."

At the grimness of his helmsman's voice, Durie hastily propelled himself across the bridge to one of the consoles. "Show me."

Boyd typed in a command. "Look at those readings."

"Run it through the computer." Durie turned his head. "Janey?"

The comm-officer shook her head. "No response to any of my signals," she announced in her New Zealand-accented voice.

"Ion engines." Boyd tapped the screen with his finger as two sets of data blinked. "We have a match."

"Damn." Durie shook his head. "Double damn."

"Devastators."

"Looks like it. Janey, open distress call on all frequencies. Boyd, full power to the engines. Get us the hell out of here."

"Initiating the 'getting the hell out of here' maneuver."

"But this is the Sol system. There aren't any Devastators around here."

Durie looked over at Janey. "There are now," he said.

* * *

"Contact lost with recon scout *Titmouse*."

Arden closed his eyes for a moment.

"Your orders, Admiral?"

"Download their last transmission, Iorillo." Arden didn't bother to open his eyes. "Alert me when you have it cleaned up."

"Yes, Sir."

Arden listened to the other officers as the station's command deck grew busier.

"Maintain alert status."

"Begin routing traffic away from that area."

"I want a full diagnostic run on all weapon batteries."

"Bring secondary reactors into standby modes."

Arden opened his eyes and turned his head to the left as the command deck's main hatch hissed open.

Trevor Ross matched his pace to that of the Prime Minister as the two men stepped onto the station's command deck. He stopped and stood near the Prime Minister's right side.

Arden kept his expression neutral.

Ross smiled with fake warmth. "Admiral Arden."

"General Ross. To what do I owe the honour?"

"The Prime Minister wished to visit central system command. As his current liaison, how could I refuse to guide him?"

"How indeed?"

"Did we come at a bad time, Admiral?"

"Is there ever a good time to visit, Prime Minister?" Arden countered. "The war is ongoing."

"And it seems to have shifted closer to home," Trudeau countered.

"That remains to be seen."

"Surely UHW Spacey is ready for a battle? You have been conducting extensive field exercises for most of the last year. You, yourself, were incommunicado for some time last month on one such *exercise*." Trudeau's eyes narrowed. "It gave us all quite a scare...as I recall."

"Admiral?"

Grateful for the distraction, Arden turned to his aide. "Yes, Iorillo?"

"We have the transmission video." He hooked his thumb towards the main monitor.

A seemingly huge ship filled the holotank. It was drifting against the stars, obscuring them with its apparent bulk. Running lights blinked across its blocky hull. Then a bright green beam lanced towards the camera recording the image and the screen turned blank with ominous quickness.

"What is that?" Trudeau asked in his calm voice.

"A fully operational Devastator factory ship."

"Here in the Sol System?"

"Yes." Arden spoke the single word in a quiet voice.

"Can we destroy it?"

"I hope so." The admiral's voice was still subdued.

General Ross cleared his throat. "Four thousand meters in length and over two and a half thousand and meters high. It's a monster with more firepower than an entire battle squadron."

"We've destroyed them before, General."

"Yes, that battleship killed one."

"The *Patton?*"

"Yes, that's the one."

Arden shook his head. "That *Patton* allowed itself to be captured and tractored just inside a factory ship. Its crew deliberately overloaded their reactor and blew up their vessel...managing to destroy the factory ship in the process." He was pretty sure that had been a fluke. *I'm not willing to order a crew on a suicide mission to try and replicate it.*

"Jankowski destroyed one at Kosbrak."

"He *crippled* one at Kosbrak, Ross," Arden clarified, "and then two more showed up to finish him off. That is not a strategy I wish to emulate."

* * *

Zane shook his head. "Not again."

The main display screen flickered and resolved. Two of the massive hulks were drifting towards the planet.

"Devastator factory ships are entering low orbit," Wolfgang announced.

"The defense forces?"

"Gone."

"There must be someone left!"

Boxleitner shook his head, his expression grim. "A handful of sub-orbital fighters maybe. A few squads of colonial marines dirt side. Nothing that can fight off one of those ships."

"My grandfather was one of the few survivors of Bonevista." Zane looked across the bridge of his frigate. "He watched the Devastators bombard the planet with their radiation cannons and biological bombs before descending upon the surface to strip-mine every last resource." He clenched his fist. "I will not lose Sirius!"

"Captain, we can't do anything to change this."

"Damn it!" Zane shook his head as Boxleitner spoke. "We have to do something! We lost Beta Durani...we can't lose this system as well."

Boxleitner was silent. *What can I say?*

Wolfgang cleared his throat. "Captain, they've started firing on the surface."

* * *

The alien blinked its ruby-red eyes. "Who are you?" It managed to speak in passable Goolatch.

"We're Humans."

"K'tok, of the Murn." The reptilian alien slapped his fists against his chest and then bowed his head. "You saved us."

The Human officer gave them a weak smile. "We could not abandon you against such odds."

"We expected to have our colony attacked by the Goolatch, not these machines."

"The machines will return." The other Murn grimaced. "They are relentless." The alien looked around the *Deliverance's* shuttle bay. "You have Ospma technology."

"Yes."

"They cannot save you."

"They cannot save themselves." K'Tok frowned. "You are their new mercenaries."

"We fight alongside the Ospma against the Devastators."

"The Devastators are brutal."

"What is that?"

"Some historical tapes from Twenty-Two Nineteen." Trudeau slumped back in his handcrafted office chair. "Memories from the past." His tie was crumpled and abandoned on the top of his desk.

"And hints at our future?"

"I hope not. The Murn lost all of their worlds in the next decade. I do not think there are any of them left alive now."

"A pity."

Trudeau sighed. "A drink?"

"Perhaps in a bit." Trevor Ross took a breath. He was carrying a small comp-pad in his hand. "Anzac Station is reporting in...heavy damage to its hull. Some sections were compromised and vented."

"Still just the one carrier on the attack?"

"Three of them now, with full drone loads."

"What ships are in that area?"

"Elements of the Thirty-Second Squadron," Ross replied without bothering to check the comp-pad. "Admiral Jarrell has already ordered them to engage."

"Hopefully this is just a feint."

"And if it's not?"

"Then we shall have a firsthand view for the destruction of Earth. And that," Trudeau commented, "is a show I would like to avoid seeing."

* * *

"We have lost the Sirius colony." Trudeau studied the faces of his Parliament with sadness. The Senate Chamber was set in a tower rising from the eastern edge of the Complex. The room itself was roughly rectangular with the seating arranged in levels. Trudeau's own chair was the end of the room, facing all the others.

So many empty seats, he thought sadly. *The room is growing too large for us.* "The Twenty-Third Battle Squadron fought valiantly, losing ninety per cent of their number before the bombardment began. The rest of the Squadron gave their lives defending the civilian convoy evacuating the colony.

"Captain Collin Zane is hereby recognized for his bravery in engaging and destroying two carriers while waiting for Kaminara Station to open a wormhole. His actions saved the lives of thousands of civilians before the beacon station was destroyed."

"This is on top of losing the last of our mining operations in Beta Durani?"

Trudeau lifted his eyes towards the seated politician. "Yes, Mister Clark."

"Captain Zane was in command of *that* defensive battle as well, was he not?"

"The captain was not the ranking officer there. He was operating as a freelance raider and gathering reconnaissance on the enemy."

"And a fine job he did of it." Clark paused for the cameras to record his expression for later broadcast. "He should have some excellent firsthand data about just how well the Devastators strip-mine a planet."

"Your comments are out of order!" Luis Santiago called out from his chair.

Trudeau kept his expression steady. *This is how democracy behaves as the world collapses,* he thought bitterly.

"Prime Minister, what about the continuing battles near the Belt?"

"The Fourteenth Calvary Squadron is continuing to skirmish with a factory ship near Ceres. First Fleet Admiral Jarrell informs me that the Devastators operating there should be hunted down and destroyed within the next three to four days."

"Is there truth to the rumours that the Devastators used non-standard locations to open their wormholes?"

"You know that answer as well as I, Mister Graw." Trudeau stared across the floor at the other Member of Parliament. "There is no method to prevent a non-standard point from being used if the other ship is willing to expend such a staggering amount of raw energy." *He's just playing up for the media.* "If someone has access to sufficiently advanced computing systems, unimaginable levels of energy, and wormhole technology, then yes non-standard locations can be used."

The room was silent.

"Are there any other questions?" Trudeau asked.

"Are the Ospma sending reinforcements?"

"Of course our allies will be sending any and all available ships to aid in our defence. The overwhelming importance—both strategic and tactical—of the Sol System is without question."

"Is there still only one factory ship?"

"As far as we can determine."

"One is still too many."

"True."

Luis Santiago shook his head. "But hopefully one ship is manageable."

"UHW Spacey is taking steps to deal with the problem."

Clark did not look convinced.

* * *

"Anna?" Felix Boxleitner stood in front of the screen watching the *'please hold'* icon blinking on and off. "Come on, pick-up."

The screen brightened. "*Hello?*" The woman brushed red hair out of her half-closed eyes as she squinted at the camera. "*Felix!*" She gave him a warm smile. "*Where are you?*"

"I'm currently stationed near Mars. Look, Anna, I've reconsidered the *Marco Polo* mission. With the Devastators attacking Sol, I think you'd be a lot safer out on the Rim. Do you have time to catch up with the *Marco Polo?*"

"*Yes, it hasn't left orbit yet. Doctor Sung was waiting to obtain final clearance from Masada Station.*"

"Then transfer onboard." He stared at her. "Please."

Anna stared back at him. "*Are you sure? This is awfully sudden for—*"

"Yes, I'm sure! Call OPE and accept the assignment." Boxleitner paused, reaching his fingers towards the image of her face. "I wish I was there to tell you this in person but we're still operating under mission orders. We could be heading back out anytime now."

"*Then should you be contacting me? Isn't this violating mission security?*"

"I don't care about that. It's not like the Devastators have ever shown any signs of tapping our transmissions before." He sighed. "You'll be out of contact as long as you're onboard that Off-Planet Expeditions ship. Hopefully you'll be safe there on the Rim. Safer than I likely am." He paused, taking a final lingering look at his wife. "I love you, Anna."

"*I love you too, Felix.*" The screen went dark.

After taking a deep breath, Boxleitner turned to his left. "Thank you, Captain."

Standing against the bulkhead, Zane simply shrugged. "I see no reason not to allow personal calls."

"I know it took a lot of power to transmit all the way to...."

"Power is cheap in the grand scheme." Zane shrugged. "We have a patrol to complete." As Boxleitner left, Zane gave the comm-console one last look of his own.

Chapter Fourteen

"Status of enemy ships?" Arden paced across the *Eye of Ra's* command deck. His magnetic shoes clicked softly at every step.

"Still closing on Mars. The defensive perimeter is being tightened." Mars had been inhabited since Twenty Ninety...the red planet would not fall quickly nor easily. "All available ships have been deployed. Admiral Jarrell is commanding that battle personally."

Arden nodded, more to himself. *He has enough of First Fleet gathered there...the planet should be safe from just about anything.* "Any word from the Ospma?"

Marcus Chapman turned around. His dark blue uniform was crisp and freshly pressed. "Their warships are assembling with our defense lines."

"What about those research ships?"

"Still in orbit around the sun, I think."

Arden was surprised. *Still in solar orbit? It's been months and months since they arrived. Hasn't it*? "Are they going to join the fight?"

"They're science vessels, Admiral. Not warships."

"They're still capable of defending themselves, right?"

"Not enough to make any difference in a major fleet battle. The Mars defense perimeter is already strongly patrolled by elements of First Fleet—only Earth itself has stronger defences. The Devastators won't break through."

"You hope."

"Yes, I do." Arden took a deep breath. "Increase speed to the main engines!" he snapped. "Get this old crate moving."

The helmsman sighed. "Engines are already at maximum, Admiral. We're already risking an overheat."

"I don't care. The battle is going to begin soon and I want to be there."

* * *

"Phobos One is off-line!"

Collin Zane winced. "We can't help them." The defensive lines were being smashed apart by the sheer weight of the Devastator fleet. "So many drones." There were far too many to count on the *Hellstorm's* displays. *At least they're fragile targets,* he thought bitterly.

The *Devastator* itself continued forward. Its immense maw glowed with raw energy, as if there was a captive sun inside the monstrous vessel.

"Break and attack!"

At Zane's order, Michael Jankowski keyed in the course while Gerald Kemp triggered the main batteries.

"Multiple hits on primary target. Reading some damage to their superstructure."

"Not enough to hurt it though."

Zane knew that even before Boxleitner spoke up. "Hit it again...we have to weaken those ray shields." Then their surge cannons and laser batteries might be able to have some effect.

Two *Torrential* missile cruisers—the *Apollo* and the *Athena*—opened fire and volleys of missiles streaked across space.

Two missiles were intercepted by drones who rammed them. The rest of the missiles impacted against the Devastator's hull with bright explosions.

"Order the *Endor* to increase its signal disruption." With strong enough jamming, the Devastator's control over its drones would be disrupted.

"Jamming already at full strength."

"Route all power to the sensors."

"Ospma ships on attack run!"

A squadron of *Battleglobes* and *Battlehexes* dove on their target.

The blocky *Devastator* seemed to ignore the first few shots, but the Ospma increased the rate of fire and the output of dozens of surge cannons raked its dark hull. Then it slowed.

"It's stopping!"

"Is it?"

Energy bolts began streaking from its defensive guns.

The mixture of green and blue is almost pretty, Zane thought as the sensors recorded the sheer amount of energy in that barrage.

One of the *Battleglobes* was hit.

Bluish energy crackled across its hull and its thrusters flared once and then went dark. A small explosion erupted from one of the now-silent surge cannons.

Green bolts of light began pelting its hull as the Devastator concentrated on it.

Moments later, the *Battleglobe* blew apart in a spectacular fireball which was quickly snuffed out.

"Scan for survivors," Zane ordered.

Wolfgang shook his head with a grimace on his face. "There won't be any life pods...not after that."

"Must have hit their reactor." Boxleitner's voice was very soft. "Catastrophic field disruption."

"The ship simply imploded." The peril of using a singularity as the power reactor for a warship.

"The Devastator is moving towards the debris."

"Damn." Zane watched as the warship debris was sucked into the factory ship's maw.

"So much for survivors." Boxleitner winced.

"And that machine will just build new weapons to throw at us." *How many of those twin ion engine fighter-drones can be built from one Battleglobe?* Zane wondered.

* * *

"Mars has held." Trudeau kept his voice steady while he made that unexpected announcement from his chair. "The defensive perimeter was nearly broken, but it held."

The room erupted into cheers.

"What were our losses?"

Trudeau didn't have an immediate response as the cheering slackened.

"Acceptable." Singh stepped forward, resplendent in full dress uniform. It was out of the ordinary for him to address Parliament, but these were extraordinary times. "We lost a number of ships, but UHW Spacey managed to destroy no less than five factory ships as well as two dozen carriers. A clear victory by any standards."

"We lost nearly ninety *Deliverances* in doing so." Clark made that comment in a cold voice. "As well as ten *Endors* and I believe seventeen *Torrential* missile cruisers."

"I believe that the losses to the Ospma were equally heavy," Santiago added.

"The cost in *Human* lives was higher than it should have been!" Clark ignored the mention of their allies. "We should have been able to stop the Devastators without losing so many ships."

"In a perfect universe, we would indeed have done so." Singh shrugged. "This is far from a perfect universe."

"I call for a motion to censure Admiral Jarrell. His Martian battle plan was wasteful. He has failed to protect the Sol System. He must be removed!"

Parliament erupted into chaos as various factions shouted in support or opposition of the motion.

"Order!" Trudeau called out. "I will have order!"

Singh leaned over as an aide hurried to his side and whispered something to him.

"You have something to add, Fleet Admiral?"

Singh looked up at Clark. "Venusian Orbital Station is taking fire," he said coldly. "A factory ship and its carrier escorts. It can't be held."

"That station was built in Twenty One Eleven. It's ancient technology."

"And now it's scrap."

"Worse, now it's resources for the Devastator."

Trudeau shook his head as a sense of despair fell over the chamber. "We have won a victory at Mars…a minor skirmish at Venus cannot be easily compared." The earlier joyful tone was lost. *Where did everything begin to go so very very wrong?*

Singh was staring at him.

* * *

Felix Boxleitner was holding a *Transcom P2050* comp-pad in his right hand. "We have confirmed the ion signatures with a passing maint-bot. Devastators sighted just around the asteroid cluster."

"How many?" Zane asked in a calm voice.

"One factory ship, multiple carriers."

"They must be replenishing their drone supplies." Boxleitner looked at his captain. "A prelude to a fresh attack against Mars Colony."

"We have to disrupt them." *Obviously.* Zane grimaced.

Felix was nodding. "What are your orders?"

"How many UHW Spacey ships in the area?"

"Just us."

"I was afraid of that."

"Most of the local patrols are holding at Mars and Io. Protecting the civilians and our colonial holdings."

"Tied down you mean." *The Admiralty is conceding most of the system to the enemy so that they can protect whatever we have left. How can we hope to win this war if no one wants to risk fighting?* Not that fighting had been all that successful so far.

"Stand by to break cover." Zane kept his voice steady. "At my signal, full power to all weapons. We charge the factory ship and hit it with everything we've got."

"A surprise assault?"

"Any objections, Commander?"

"Just the way I like it," Boxleitner replied.

"Call for reinforcements. I don't want to make this a suicide mission."

"I'll see to it."

"One carrier disabled."

"Interceptors are overheating!" Gerald Kemp swore loudly as his console sparked. The surge cannons were being used to shoot drones out of the sky as fast as they could recharge.

"Range on the factory ship?" Zane demanded.

"Closing now."

"Fire surge cannons as you bear, fire missile racks when their shields weaken."

"Aye, Captain."

"Where are my reinforcements?"

"No contact yet."

Boxleitner watched the displays flicker. "One carrier destroyed, one crippled."

"Leave it for later."

"We're experiencing an energy surge from the reactor."

"Monitor it." Zane cursed softly. *I won't be blown up by my own ship!* he vowed. "If we're having energy surges, shunt that extra power into the weaponry and make use of it."

"Aye, Captain."

"Closing on the factory ship," Jankowski announced.

"Fire as we bear." Zane winced. The target was huge. "Should be impossible to miss it."

"I know, Captain."

"Energy spike from target!"

"Go evasive!" Zane shouted but the *Hellstorm* was hit!

The light panels flared and the ship's bulkheads groaned. A pipe in the ceiling ruptured and sparks showered onto the deck as metallic debris clattered off the bulkheads.

Alert klaxons sounded.

"Captain?" Boxleitner turned in his chair.

Zane was sprawled limply in his chair, blood flowing from a scalp wound.

"Medical team to the bridge!" Boxleitner shouted into his comm.

The frigate shuddered again as additional laser bolts raked its hull.

"I'm assuming command," Boxleitner announced. "Ship status?"

"Thrusters offline," Jankowski said.

"Weapons are down." Kemp slammed his hands onto his console. "Come on, guys!"

"We're crippled." Wolfgang shook his head. "Damage reports coming in from all the over the ship."

"Drones have broken off their attacks. We're still moving."

"Course?" Boxleitner already knew the answer.

Jankowski swallowed. "Right towards the factory ship."

"Damn."

"UHW Spacey squadron hailing us...unable to respond. The transmitter array is offline."

"ETA of the squadron?"

"Thirty-five minutes."

"How long until we get consumed?"

"Twenty-two minutes."

"Great." Boxleitner shook his head. "Repair times?"

"No idea, Sir."

"Focus on thrusters and weapons. We have to try and delay our impending destruction."

"Should we abandon ship?"

"No point, Wolfgang. The drones will cut the life pods to pieces. Damn, I wish we had a working weapon."

Kemp was still tapping buttons on his console but there was no apparent response. "I'm just glad the warheads weren't set off."

Boxleitner frowned. "Warheads?"

"Our missiles."

"That's it!"

"Sir?"

Boxleitner was smiling now. "We still have nukes, right?"

Kemp nodded. "Three missiles, but the launching system is down."

"Get the warheads to the hanger bay."

The hatch opened and two medical corpsmen floated onto the bridge.

"See to the captain." Boxleitner turned back to Kemp. "Get those warheads down to the hanger bay," he repeated, "and then see if you can scare up some maneuvering thrusters from a space suit."

Kemp frowned. "Aye, Sir." His tone betrayed his confusion with the orders.

"I have a plan. I hope it works." Boxleitner tapped at his comm. "Flight deck, come in."

"Flight deck here."

"This is Boxleitner. I need volunteers in the hanger bay immediately."

"Are we going to evac—"

"No, we're going to save the *Hellstorm*. And ourselves."

Chapter Fifteen

"The worst of the fighting seems to have died down for now. However, heavy raiding and probing attacks continue to occur throughout the system."

Dale Arden looked across the display table at the other people present. Most were technical staff operating the room's assorted equipment, but many of the remaining Joint Chiefs were also present as was an Ospma and several Members of Parliament. "I would almost call the current situation a stalemate." He directed his words towards Prime Minister Trudeau. Flashing lights on the table drew his attention before Trudeau could respond. "What's that, Carter?"

"Another probing attack against Mars is underway." The officer held his hand to his headset. "A carrier-based force, no factory ships."

Ashvim Singh cleared his throat. "I have every confidence in Admiral Jarrell's ability to defend that world."

Trudeau frowned.

"I never suggested otherwise." Arden turned back to the table and only then took a deep breath. *Singh is getting on my nerves,* he thought. *That man wants power and he'll stop at nothing to get it. Even with the United Human Worlds dying around him.*

Singh stepped away from a console where an Ospma had coiled itself. "Do we have any firm numbers on the in-system strength of the Devastators?"

Jennifer Romano tilted her head.

"Nothing definite as yet." Lee Hwan Kim's voice was soft, yet an underlying sense of resignation was present. "I believe that we have engaged and destroyed in excess of two hundred carriers and seventeen factory ships in the last month."

Arden shook his head in seeming disbelief. *A staggering victory by any means surely!*

"The number of drone fighters we've destroyed is simply impossible to count. Certainly in the *thousands*."

"With UHW Spacey having lost one hundred and forty-three *Deliverances* so far," the Honourable Morgan Clark commented in a sour tone of voice. "Twenty-six *Endor* frigates and fifty-two *Torrential* missile cruisers have been destroyed or crippled. The death toll to military personnel alone is over a hundred thousand in just this system."

Anton Trudeau smiled grimly at his wife as she gasped at Clark's words. "You wanted to join me at work," he said to her in a soft tone of voice.

"These could be the last days of humanity," Isabelle replied. She wore a floor-length green gown, with a bright red shawl wrapped around her shoulders. "My place is at your side."

"And you are most welcome there."

Singh cleared his throat. "This command centre is no place for civilians," he said gruffly. "It should be restricted to military personnel only."

"The entire system is a battlefield, Admiral Singh...where else will I be any safer?" Isabelle glared back at him, pointedly ignoring Clark's glare at her, and then calmly reached into a pocket in her skirt and removed a *Transcom P2050* comp-pad. She activated it and proceeded to read the text scrolling across its screen.

Ashvim Singh blinked his brown eyes at being so studiously ignored.

"So many carriers and even a thousand fighters is an outstanding kill ratio for any conflict in this long war." Arden tried to bring the meeting back on track. "Even with our own losses—"

"We've lost too many!" Clark argued.

"Half of UHW Spacey's fleet is gone." Kim looked across the room, which had gone silent. "*Half!*" he repeated in a soft tone of voice. "And the Devastators are still coming."

Romano tossed her own comp-pad onto a table. "The governmental Complex will likely be a primary target. We will need to assemble a strong garrison."

"General Romano that would be true against a conventional enemy. We're fighting a rather non-conventional foe."

She snorted. "Prime Minister, my ground pounders have given a good accounting of themselves on every front so far. When," she amended, "they have been allowed to fight."

"And they've been wiped out in every campaign so far." Singh made that comment. "Last man fights are not helping morale."

"Neither will endless retreats. I will not order my troops to abandon civilians to this or any other enemy. They would not obey such orders in any event." She glared at the other officers. "We're going to fight for every world the United Human Worlds claims and that is final."

"The Devastators are too numerous and relentless."

"What do you suggest we do, Clark?"

Arden nodded. "We've junked hundreds of their ships during the war. We've got the firepower in our home system to make any attacks far too costly for them to win."

"Hundreds destroyed...and hundreds more will come," a harsh voice rasped out. "This system is a nexus." Essan coiled one of his arms around a control pad as the Humans looked at him. "Many wormholes open from here into the greater network."

"And the Devastators know this?" Trudeau asked.

"They must suspect." Kim closed his eyes. "If they have decrypted even the most basic civilian navigational database, they would know the importance of Earth."

"We should recall Admirals Ivanova and Wassen. With Second and Third Fleets to assist, we can drive the Devastators from this system."

Trudeau looked at Singh, his eyes narrowing. "Or lose the territory guarded by those fleets."

Singh shook his head. "Prime Minister, the bulk of the Devastators' military strength *must* be committed against the Sol System."

"And what do you base that conclusion on?"

Singh grimaced. "The sheer number of enemy vessels currently marauding through our home system. Far more factory ships than have ever been committed to any other system during the recorded history of this war."

"Military Intelligence has no firm idea on the overall military strength of our foe," Kim protested. "Nor do our Ospma allies."

Essan said nothing. His tentacle-arms simply waved slowly as if in an underwater current.

"The Devastators are a nomadic race attacking us without hesitation or mercy. They come to strip our worlds of resources." Arden looked at the other officers in turn. "We must fight to the death of one species or the other."

"These are machines, not a real lifeform." Singh waved his hand dismissively. "They cannot hope to overcome the strength of humanity."

Isabelle Trudeau shook her head at his tone.

* * *

"That certainly was an innovative tactic, Commander."

"Thank you, Sir." Felix Boxleitner nodded his head. "I had to do something."

"You did better than I would have. I think." Collin Zane's gaze flicked back to a visual display which was replaying the end of the battle. "Very interesting tactic, I must say." A bandage was wrapped across his forehead and his face was still paler than usual.

The *Hellstorm* was drifting slowly towards the gaping maw of a factory ship. The cavernous opening was glowing like a star, a raging furnace ready to burn the frigate to ash.

Three small objects streaked from the *Hellstorm's* hanger bay and accelerated towards the factory ship.

"Yes, most innovative."

Powerful explosions erupted from within the opening.

The star-like glow flared more brightly and then went dark.

Boxleitner cleared his throat. "We managed to cripple it long enough for our reinforcements to arrive. Their missile cruisers finally managed to finish it off."

So close to destruction, Zane thought. *Saved by what must be considered to be have been sheer luck.* "Repair status to the *Hellstorm*?"

"The ship is combat worthy under emergency conditions, Captain. Full repairs will require a stay in an actual shipyard, though, so that might be a while in coming."

"We'll settle for what we can manage ourselves. There's no time to park in a shipyard. The Spacey needs every ship capable of fighting to be out on the front lines."

"The crew know that."

Zane snorted. "I know they know that." He paused for a moment, looking uncertain of how to continue. "You did a good job while I was unconscious. Glad to have you aboard."

"Glad to have been here, Sir."

* * *

"Any fresh readings, Barstow?" Admiral Janice Sawyer kept her voice calm even though her stomach was churning.

Scott Barstow shook his head. "The attack force is closing on the station. It looks like two factory ships on approach, with heavy drone support. Possibly some other escorting carriers."

"They just appeared on our sensors...popped out of nowhere."

Barstow nodded. "Their damned propulsion system is superior to ours."

"We'll debate it later. Let's use what warning time we do have. Alert Earth Central and request reinforcements. Sound battle stations." The crew of *Masada* Station was already at a level of alert, so the klaxon was little more than a reminder to snap to attention. "Seal the interior bulkheads." It was a given that the hull would be breached during the coming battle...pre-sealing the bulkheads would limit damage and atmosphere loss.

"All decks report combat ready."

"Escort ships are forming up...awaiting your orders."

"Clear them to advance...try to slow the enemy approach." Sawyer wished that she had more warships stationed at *Masada,* but most of her usual escorts had been diverted on another mission. *I just have to make do with the ones I do still have.*

"We're getting inquiries from the civilians."

"Order them to scatter, Mason." *Damn them!* Admiral Sawyer studied a display, taking note of how focused her crew were on their duties. *Masada* was the Sol System's nadir transit station and controlled the wormholes for civilian and military traffic. There were a lot of ships waiting near the station to make transit. "Do they have time to get clear?"

"Unlikely for most of them." Barstow gestured to the approaching Devastators. "They'll be intercepted before they can escape."

Sawyer winced. *They're too slow to escape.* The Devastators would rip those unarmed hulls apart. "Sato, open a wormhole and get as many of them out of here as you can. Maybe they'll be safe at Orion."

"That will divert power from our weapons."

"I know that." *What other choice do we have?* "How long until the Devastators arrive?"

"Factory ships will enter weapons range in twenty minutes. Those drones will be here in five or so."

"Opening a vortex."

"Get the civilians clear. And do it fast."

"Eight carriers closing on our position."

"Priority order: escorts are to provide cover fire for the civilians. *Masada* will have to stand on its own for now." Sawyer cleared her throat. "All gun crews, stand by."

"The carriers are launching more drones."

The tactical display lit up with hundreds of icons as they spilled from the blocky warships.

"Damn, there's a lot of them."

"Orders?"

Sawyer raised her voice to carry across the command deck. "ECM on maximum. Try to jam their control frequencies." It was a tactic that seldom worked for long, but it was worth trying.

"Transmitters online."

"Civilians are still escaping."

Sawyer noted the number of freighters still waiting for a chance to enter the wormhole. They weren't panicking yet, but she knew it would come once the first strafing runs began. "We have to hold the drones off then. All batteries, fire at will!"

Individual surge cannons began drawing power from the singularity at the heart of the station and firing off electrical discharges. Each impact would cause damage, as well as secondary electrical disturbances which would propagate through the ship.

Dozens of drones exploded as their reactors overloaded. Others were simply left drifting after their guidance systems were fried.

"Target that carrier."

"Aye, Admiral."

Three electromagnetic bolters locked and fired packets of charged particles towards one of the carriers. Explosions lit up one of its wings as one of the powerful guns hit.

The station shuddered as two drones slipped past the defensive fire and impacted against the hull.

"Hull breach...damage control is responding."

"I hate suicide ships."

"They're not piloted craft...and they do more damage when ramming than their weapons do."

"And the factory ships just recycle all of the wreckage."

"Evacuation status?"

"We need more time!"

"We don't have it, Sato." Sawyer looked for her escorts...all three of her *Deliverances* were fighting, but drones were swarming all of them.

"Carrier two is closing fast!" Barstow saw the icons. "More drones incoming!"

"Gunners!"

"Surge cannons are running hot, Admiral."

"Energy spike!"

The station rocked.

"Heavy damage."

"We've lost the vortex!"

Glancing at a display, Sawyer saw the wormhole ripple, then implode. "No!" she cried out as three freighters were caught within the event horizon and crushed. "Scatter the rest!" she shouted.

Two of the carriers and dozens of drones moved towards the waiting freighters and began firing.

Freighters and other ships began to explode.

"Damn it!" Sawyer cursed. "We have to do something!"

"They're out of range." Barstow stumbled away from the tactical station as *Masada* shuddered again. "The escorts are over-stretched."

"I can see that."

"Factory ships are entering extreme range!"

"Continue firing!"

One of the resonance generators charged and fired a fan-shaped glowing beam which swept across the hull of one carrier.

Sawyer grimaced. "With luck, that will disrupt something important." The generator used opposing electromagnetic fields to set up resonating vibrations in the affected ship...the vibrations only lasted a few moments, but the resulting shockwaves could cause significant damage as they reverberated throughout the ship.

A Devastator factory ship fired a volley of energy bolts back.

Chapter Sixteen

"How bad was it?" Arden listened to the voice through his headset.

Anton Trudeau stared at him. Arden's office was not as comfortable as his own, and lacked the windows overlooking the Green Well. *But then, it is designed for a military officer.* "Well?" he asked when the admiral took off the private-comm headset and handed it back to his aide.

Arden looked at him grimly. "The Devastators have just hit the nadir transit station."

Trudeau's eyes widened and his face paled.

"The entire Devastator battle group has been destroyed, but *Masada* Station itself was crippled and the evacuation was disrupted."

"Oh God, the civilian convoys!"

"Exactly." Arden shook his head. "Rescue and repair operations are already getting underway, but it's a daunting task. There's a lot of wreckage." He could not begin to imagine the amount of debris such a battle would have left. "Fleet losses were extremely heavy. The Joint Chiefs don't have any accurate info as yet though, so it's still just wild guesses and estimates. It's hard to know just how many civilians managed to escape and how many stayed and tried to get away and were destroyed."

"That's disastrous." Trudeau was stunned.

"I know."

The Prime Minister stared blankly at the wall, not seeing the pictures or charts hanging on it.

"*Masada* is—was—heavily armed its firepower was more than even the factory ships could withstand. Both of them were destroyed, the second one was trying to consume *Masada* when the station's singularity imploded."

Arden sighed. "Even killing a dozen factory ships doesn't make up for the Station. We still have *Leonidas* and the Joint Chiefs have ordered reinforcements there to guard it."

"If we lose *Leonidas*, we'll be unable to control the wormholes."

"Exactly. The fleets here would effectively be trapped." Some Ospma warships had integral worm-engines, but most did not and most UHW Spacey ships did not.

"The Ospma would never tolerate that."

"Oh, I agree. The Ospma would come and help us to rebuild the stations, but it would take time and resources we can ill afford."

"The Devastators are clever...they force us to tie down large numbers of our warships in a defensive posture."

"The defensive posture won't last for long. The fight will continue."

"True enough." *What other choice do we have?* Arden thought.

* * *

"This situation is intolerable!" Aki Hidoshi stared across the Chamber's floor. "Absolutely intolerable."

"For once I agree with my fellow Member." Morgan Clark kept his voice steady and calm as he rose to his feet to address his fellows. His suit coat was a dark colour of fine cloth and looked freshly ironed and immaculate. "The destruction of *Masada* Station poses a direct threat to planetary security. Steps must be taken to safeguard this planet."

Anton Trudeau blinked as the voices of Parliament rose in agreement. *This cannot be good,* he thought. *Not good at all.*

"What would you recommend then?" Admiral Dale Arden countered from his chair. His voice was equally calm and steady, matching that of the Member of Parliament. "We are already in a state of war with the Devastators. We have been operating under emergency measures and martial law since the first ships entered the Sol System."

"I would start with a full draft to mobilize every able-bodied person into UHW Spacey."

Trudeau shook his head at the thought. *The outrage would be calamitous. The citizens would revolt!*

"We don't have enough ships if we drafted ever able-bodied person." Arden pointed that out in his usual calm tone. Despite the remaining shipyards labouring around the clock, current production was barely keeping up with ongoing combat losses. "And a ground-based army is a waste of resources. This particular enemy doesn't bother with landing ground troops."

Clark gestured. "I demand that the Joint Chiefs recall all of our far-flung Fleets. We need every ship in UHW Spacey brought home to defend this planet."

"Every ship?"

Clark turned to face another Member. "Yes, Vederman."

"You would leave our remaining colonies vulnerable and helpless?"

"We can't keep them safe," Clark snarled from his chair. "Earth is the mother world...its safety must take full precedence."

"Impossible."

"Vederman, you have no real standing. Your colony is gone."

Vederman's face purpled. "And *yours* might be next, Clark."

"Gentlemen!" Trudeau took a deep breath after his shout. "Calm yourself. We must maintain decorum." He paused, but neither man said anything else. "The casualties from *Masada* are hideous. The cost is still being calculated."

"Indeed," Hidoshi agreed from his chair. "Any further civilian losses are unacceptable. We are reliant upon *Leonidas*."

"*Leonidas* has been the target of minor raids for months now. The bulk of civilian traffic chose to use the seemingly ignored *Masada*."

"Which turned out to be a trap." Elisabeth Levy did not mask the contempt in her voice. Her face was grim.

"A trap no one spotted."

"Indeed." Clark raised his voice again. "Admiral Kim has much to answer for."

Vederman shook his head.

"*Masada's* fall cost us. The loss of the station is nothing compared to the civilian lives lost."

"Some ships got away!"

"Not enough, Levy."

"Might I remind you that we are at war," Arden said. "Lives are lost everyday in this war. It has been the nature of the conflict since First Contact."

"It cannot go on!"

"No, Hidoshi, it can't! The United Human Worlds are dying."

"What do you suggest then, Levy? Should we abandon the fight and simply allow the Devastators to consume us along with our world?"

"There is certainly no possibility of surrendering to this enemy."

"The possibility of running away remains."

"Running away?" Trudeau stared across the chamber at the Honourable Member of Parliament Graw.

"Yes." That man nodded his gray-haired head calmly, despite the buzz of background chatter which was quickly filling the room. "Evacuation." The buzz grew louder. "*Masada* is crippled, not destroyed. It can be rebuilt, but *Leonidas* is still fully operational. We concede the planet to the Devastators and we flee into deep space...eventually we'll find a new world to settle on."

Trudeau was speechless at the suggestion. His mouth opened and closed a few times, and then the room erupted into protests.

"Cowardice!"

"Impossible!"

"We don't have the ships for that!"

"You can't expect us to simply wander out into the galaxy and find a habitable world." Arden shook his head at the absurdity of the thought. "There just aren't that many viable worlds out there." *How long would we have to wander? How many ships would we lose? Is Humanity fated to become a wandering race of nomads always running from the Devastators?*

Arden looked at the Member with contempt on his face. "Let alone living planets not already claimed or colonized by some other power. Would you have us become a race or nomads? Or worse? Pirates who stole an entire world?"

"How could be hide another world?" Vederman demanded. "Sooner or later, the Devastators would find your *New Earth* as well!"

"We cannot evacuate the Earth." Trudeau shook his head. "We don't have the cargo capacity to evacuate more than a fraction of the citizens living here." He could barely entertain the notion. "I will not be the head of any government operating some damnable lottery to choose who will be allowed to run and who will be left behind."

"I never suggested that *you* would be."

Trudeau stared at the Member of Parliament.

Luis Santiago rose to his feet. "My fellow Member raises a valid point...at what point do we admit that this is a lost battle and retreat?"

"Member Santiago, I will not be remembered by history as the Prime Minister who oversaw the destruction of Humanity."

Assuming, Arden thought into the sudden grim silence, *that anyone survives to write such a history.* The survival of any race was looking more and more unlikely.

* * *

"Felix?" Collin Zane keyed open the hatch with his override code and then peered into the dark quarters. "Felix? Are you in here?"

A figure was sitting on the bed in near-complete darkness.

Zane stepped inside and the hatch hissed closed behind him. "What's wrong? You're late for your duty shift and not answering your comm."

The figure waved a hand listlessly towards the wall monitor and otherwise did not acknowledge the captain's presence.

Zane squinted. Names were scrolling across the display at a steady rate. He recognized them quickly enough. "The casualty report from *Masada*?" He frowned. "Why are you reading them over?" One named suddenly caught his eye. "*Marco Polo*."

"The *Marco Polo*," Boxleitner said brokenly, "was attempting to transit out-system when the Devastators arrived. The ship was destroyed with all hands. No one escaped. No life pods have been recovered."

Zane's eyes widened. "My God." He stood there, uncertain what else to say.

"No one survived," Boxleitner whispered.

* * *

It is good to be back. If there is going to be an attack, then I want to be here to defend my station. Brad Chambers stared through the window of the shuttle as the craft flew back towards his command. The *Deliverance*-class cruiser, *Thoth's Wisdom*, moved to join the other warships overseeing civilian liners and freighters as they moved towards the station.

Leonidas Station was surrounded by warships, and by military freighters labouring to emplace the new weapon platforms.

Each of the standard OWPs had two missile racks and two surge cannons mounted on it.

"What a waste of money."

"Oh?" Brad turned to look at his shuttle pilot.

"Two hundred and fifty megadollars to build one of those things."

"The added defense will be nice though. Less than a month ago, the Devastators hit *Masada* with overwhelming force. I don't mind having more OWPs and larger minefields set into place to protect us."

"Too much junk will just clutter the shipping lanes."

"We have transponders and control over the weaponry." Brad could see no serious dangers. "I don't see there being any risk of friendly fire."

"You hope." The pilot snorted. "Look at that monstrousity."

"The heavy OWP?" Brad was admiring it as the shuttle flew past. "Four missile racks and two laser cannon to hit enemy ships at long-range, with four surge cannon for close in defence. It's a beautiful piece of work."

"And seven hundred megadollars apiece. You can build a cruiser for that kind of money."

"The OWPs are necessary. We can't tie down a cruiser flotilla to defend the station. Not for any serious length of time anyway. Better to have the cruisers being mobile and off hunting the enemy."

"If you look at it that way."

"I do." Brad smiled. "Give me a dozen of these beauties and I could hold off a factory ship."

"Let's hope we don't have to test that theory."

* * *

"The independent freighter lines are transiting out-system as quickly as they can through *Leonidas*. The civilian evacuation continues."

Ashvin Singh snorted. He was seated in one plush arm-chair, clearly uncomfortable. "That evacuation is draining resources we could better employ against the invaders."

"The civilians are on the edge of panic," Dale Arden countered. He seemed at ease in his chair. The Prime Minister's office was supposed to be neutral ground for them, putting them at their ease. *It's not working.*

Singh took a sip from his coffee mug.

"The civilians only see the Devastators coming and know that UHW Spacey is barely slowing them," Arden said. "Every news report tells of another station or minor colony lost."

"The Skywalker Military Base was not worth mentsrouning."

"Someone obviously thought that it was." Cynthia Randall spoke up. "It was a headline story."

"Must have been a slow news day." Singh did not mask the contempt in his voice. "The newscasts obviously aren't of much help to us."

"No, but a free press is vital to maintaining what little morale we still have. What are your thoughts, Prime Minister?"

Anton Trudeau stood by the window and didn't reply to Cynthia's question. He was staring down into the Green Well.

Arden stared at his back, but didn't say anything.

"At least reports from our colonies are fairly steady now," Cynthia continued. "The wild swings from victory to defeat are settling down."

"I don't like it."

"Admiral Singh? You don't like it that not one of our remaining colonies is reporting contact with any Devastators? Are you insane?"

Trudeau turned his head around. "If there are no Devastators out there, Mrs Randall, then where did they all go?"

"Prime Minister?"

Dale Arden gave a start as his PDA buzzed. He hastily read the message scrolling across the tiny monitor. "We have another scouting report...another flotilla of Devastators has just transited into the zenith point."

"How many?" Anton Trudeau turned completely away from the Green Well and towards the other people gathered in his office. The walls were lined with monitors—normally hidden behind carved wooden paneling—several of which were showing tactical-style displays of the system.

"Nine factory ships this time." Arden kept his voice calm, though it cracked a bit with tension.

"With carrier support?" They always came with carrier support.

"We estimate ten to fourteen carriers per Devastator."

"This must be planning towards their final push against us." Ashvim Singh sounded pleased. "We knew that they would come in force...this must be their full strength."

"Be that as it may," Arden spoke up, "we cannot continue to hold out against such massive firepower. We are stretched far too thin."

"We have no choice. This is the Sol System, not some expendible colony world." Trudeau turned back towards the Green Well. "We have no other choice."

Chapter Seventeen

Marcus Chapman planted his magnetic-soled shoes more firmly on the deck of his bridge. "We have an urgent report from *Sea Witch*—a Lockheed-Rollings freighter. They confirm that a Devastator battle group is moving towards *Leonidas*."

"We will intercept them."

"You hope."

"We *will* intercept them short of the station." Dale Arden kept his tone light, as the rest of the *Eye of Ra's* bridge crew worked their stations in nervous silence. "We have the firepower to spare."

"What about the second fleet reportedly moving towards Earth?"

"We have lots of warships there as well. The orbital defence grid will blast the Devastators out of the sky faster than their factory ships can build replacements."

Chapman frowned. "You sound confident."

"I am." Arden smiled. *I have to be.*

* * *

Anton Trudeau turned from the window into the Green Well towards his guest. "Have you seen the latest reports, Gorpshan?"

The Ospma made no verbal reply, though his tentacle-arms waved in a seemingly meaningless manner. He sat—crouched—in the centre of the carpet, not bothering with any of the chairs.

"Fleet scouts have observed thirty more wormholes opening in the last three weeks. *Thirty*! Devastators continue to enter the system in great numbers."

"Anticipated."

Trudeau stared at him. "Anticipated? How can you say that so calmly? Why weren't we informed of this attack?"

Gorpshan said nothing.

"Have you seen this particular report?" Singh called up a visual. That particular Devastator was massive, dwarfing the other factory ships. "I've never seen one so big."

Gorpshan's mouthparts clicked softly.

Trudeau stared at the image. "It's huge."

"The Prime Factory."

Trudeau turned to stare at his ally with a frown. "The *what*?"

"It is rumoured," Gorpshan rasped, "by some races, that the first of these factory ships appeared from beyond the Rim. That one ship devastated many worlds and converted their resources into new factory ships and other warships."

Singh gestured. "Prime Minister, we do have evidence that these Devastators actually *grow* larger over time, converting resources into new equipment and superstructure. If that is the case, then this particular Devastator is truly ancient."

"And powerful?"

"That goes without saying."

Gorpshan waved his arms. "A chance exists for us to win this war." His mauve-coloured skin mottled with waves of lilac.

"Which would be how?"

"A final battle. Destroy all and none will be left to threaten us."

"But can we be certain that we do destroy them all?" Trudeau demanded. "From what I understand, if even just one factory ship escapes, it will replicate itself back into a fleet. Eventually."

"An option exists."

"What option?"

"Costly, but cheaper than defeat."

"Will the Ospma Baronies be sending more of their fleets to support us?" Singh demanded.

The Ospma lurched into motion towards the door.

"Gorpshan?"

"Final victory comes. Be prepared."

Trudeau and Singh watched the Ospma undulate out of the office. The two men exchanged looks. "Well, that went as well as it usually does."

Singh snorted.

* * *

"So what options do we have?" Gerald Kemp asked.

"Delaying tactics are pretty much all that we have left to us." Collin Zane grimaced as the *Hellstorm's* tactical display updated itself with current estimates of enemy positions. "Against so many ships..."

"We won't give up easily. They're going to burn."

"I know, Boxleitner." The captain's eyes narrowed as he studied his executive officer. *He's gotten too grim, too focused on revenge. He should be relieved of duty for a time.* But all of UHW Spacey was strapped for trained crews right now and the current crisis allowed no one any time for grief. *Better to work out his anger in battle, then sulk alone down on Earth.*

Michael Jankowski looked up from his console. "Do you think the Wolf Shipyards will be sending any reinforcements?"

"I hope so." Zane kept his tone optomistic. "I can't see why Admiral Webber wouldn't launch fresh ships as soon as they can clear their slips." Surely UHW Spacey would be scrambling to get every last one of its ships—even the most remotely combatworthy hull—into action.

"We're going to need more assistance from the Ospma."

"*That* is a given." Kemp snorted.

"So where are our allies?" Jankowski turned to look directly at his commander. "The bulk of the Devastators are *here*...where are our allies?"

"That is a matter for the Joint Chiefs and the Prime Minister."

Boxleitner said nothing.

Zane grimaced. "I wish I had answers for you, but I do—"

"Captain!" Christoph Wolfgang interrupted, "we have an incoming distress signal from Hunter's Moon station. They're under attack."

Of course they are. Zane raised his voice. "Intercept course, Jankowski. Maximum burn. Wolfgang, signal the rest of the battle group to accompany us. Sound battle stations."

"Another skirmish."

"Yes, Felix, another skirmish."

"Good," Boxleitner said.

Zane frowed at him.

* * *

"These are just probing attacks." Arden paced along the corridor of Freedom Station at a steady pace. "They're sending small strike forces against our fortifications to wear us down. Weaken our array of defensive satellites. Tie up our mobile units defending our remaining colonies and habitats. Probe for weaknesses they can later overwhelm."

"And it appears to be working for them."

Arden made no comment.

Anton Trudeau smiled grimly at his friend's expression. "I do read my daily military reports, you know. Well, eventually."

"As well you should."

"Captain Zane held the LaGrange Five habitats?"

Arden nodded absently at a pair of passing technicians. "Most of them...with moderate losses to his battle group."

"'Moderate losses' are still too high."

"Every UHW Spacey officer knows the risks of this war."

"I know," Trudeau agreed. *And the civilians are paying too much of the cost in this damned war.*

The hatch hissed open and they stepped onto Freedom Station's command deck.

Trudeau studied the officers and technicians who worked at the multi-level room's computer stations and plotting tanks. *So many young people working so hard to defend us.* How could anyone not feel pride at this sight?

A dark-skinned man approached them with a welcoming smile. "Welcome to Freedom Station, Prime Minister. Admiral Arden."

"General Franklin." Arden nodded to the other officer.

General Richard Franklin looked tired. His uniform was still neatly pressed and crisp and he was wearing a few of his numerous medals. "The defences are holding."

"So I see." Trudeau gave the command deck another examination. "Your staff are doing a fine job."

"I've been in UHW Spacey for over fifty years, Prime Minister. I've served in a dozen major conflicts, fought the Devastators for most of my life. I have learned one thing from all that pain, all that warfare." His voice hardened. "They do not surrender and neither does UHW Spacey."

"I am glad to hear you say that."

Arden nodded. "The Joint Chiefs have their full confidence in you."

"No, they don't." Franklin shook his head, mostly in resignation. "Singh would be quite happy to have me replaced by someone more in line with his own thinking. Unfortunately, my reputation prevents him from plotting to openly against me."

"The Joint Chiefs don't have time to plot or scheme against their fellows." Arden kept his voice low. "You know that, Richard."

"Do you really believe that, Dale?"

Trudeau wandered towards a console where a young blonde technician was only too happy to explain her assigned tracking duties.

"Freedom Station is your command," Arden told him. "No one is going to relieve you."

"The war is getting worse. A lot worse. The Ospma aren't supporting us as much as they could be."

"The Devastators press everyone."

"That's bull and you know it! The bulk of the Devastator fleet is *here*!" Franklin's voice cracked. "Every factory ship loose in the galaxy must be gathering in this system. Have you seen the number of ships mining the asteroid belt?"

"Yes, I've been watching the intelligence reports. I have sources outside the Joint Chiefs."

"From outside UHW Spacey?"

Arden paused a moment, then nodded. "Yes," he admitted.

"I thought we had limited contact aside from the Ospma?"

"Officially we do."

"Ah, the perks of command."

A technician hurried towards the two officers. "General Franklin, we're being hailed."

"By whom, Lieutenant?"

"It's from a freighter following beacon two three six. Civilian registry..." he raised his hand to his headset. "Damn, we've just lost the signal."

"What?"

"They've gone silent. No response to our hails."

"What was their message?"

"They had a sensor contact, but were unable to clearly identify it."

"General Franklin," another technician called out, "we have vessels closing! Energy emissions are consistent with Devastator drones."

Franklin's face had turned a pale shade of mocha. "Sound battle stations."

Trudeau hurried back towards them as an alarm began sounding. "An attack?"

"A small probing raid." Arden gestured towards a monitor. "Mostly drones it looks like, maybe one or two carriers. Not strong enough to break through the defence grid."

"Another raid."

"It does look that way, Prime Minister." Franklin's mouth twisted sourly. "Plot their vectors!" he snapped at his aides. "Estimate targets."

"They seem to be concentrating on this station." Trudeau made that comment in a low tone. From the tactical displays, the drones were vectoring directly towards the orbital station.

Dale Arden nodded. "Freedom *is* one of the larger habitats in orbit." It was the oldest of mankind's space stations. Parts of one module were the original Freedom Station, built in the early Twenty-First Century. "We have sufficient surge cannons to engage them." To say nothing of the mobile ships in the area.

"Seal interior bulkheads!" Franklin ordered. "Route power to all weapon batteries. I want those drones destroyed before they can open fire."

"Civilian ships are scattering."

"Weapon platforms coming online!"

"Minefield now active. IFF scanning for transponder beacons."

"The *Duan Gung* is moving to engage."

"Network me with the commanders of Second Fleet." Franklin hurried towards the comm-centre. "We need to work up a strategy."

"Local elements of First Fleet are requesting orders."

"A wasteful attack," Arden commented to the prime minister as Franklin hurried away, issuing orders in a loud voice. "The Devastators are just throwing these ships away."

"You said it earlier. They want to weaken us...wear us down so they can strip the Earth of resources."

"Minefield engaged," a technician called out. "Multiple detonations detected."

"The minefields are too light to stop many drones," Franklin explained in a low tone. "They're great for slowing capital ships, but the drones are too fast for most of the mines to detect and engage. They just blow their way through ignoring whatever losses they do take."

"We need larger fields, to have more depth?"

"That would be helpful, Prime Minister, but it still won't be enough to slow a serious Devastator attack."

"Then what would?"

"A thousand more ships would be a nice start." Franklin chuckled grimly. "A little humour."

"Very little." Trudeau turned to watch a monitor. "Those drones are getting closer." There were a lot of little lights blinking on the screen.

"Weapon platforms engaging targets."

"The heavy OWPs won't be able to use their laser batteries against the drones, but their missiles and surge cannons can destroy them."

"And their carriers?"

"They appear to holding back," Arden pointed to a display. The carrier icons were clearly holding position. "They're staying out past the minefield."

"The *Duan Gung* is keeping them busy?" Trudeau frowned. "That means *Short Bow* doesn't it?"

"Well, it *is* a *Torrential* missile cruiser."

"The carriers won't last long against its firepower."

"No, they won't."

"Elements of the First Fleet are moving on intercept vectors."

"I want to know how they got so close to us." Franklin sounded furious. "Where the hell were our patrols?"

Arden shook his head. "I don't know." *Our patrols should have spotted them before they got this close. Do they have some kind of cloaking technology we haven't encountered yet? Or were they just lucky?*

"Drones entering weapons range."

"Shunting power to surge cannons!"

Franklin walked to the centre of the command deck, snapping orders. "Fire all batteries as the enemy enters our range."

The ceiling lights dimmed.

"We're taking fire,"Arden explained calmly. "The weapon batteries are requiring more power."

Trudeau looked at him. "Don't we have enough power for everything?"

"Yes, most of the time." The singularity powering the station was quite strong after all.

"Energy spikes!"

"They're firing?"

"Yes." Arden nodded. As an experienced spacer, he could feel slight vibrations in the deck plates which indicated distant impacts. His eyes sought out the station status display and took note of flashing icons. *No serious hits as yet.*

"We're taking fire!"

"Don't worry, Prime Minister. The outer hull should be able to handle the impacts from those small weapons. If not...well, that is why the interior bulkheads were sealed."

"How can you be so damned calm?" Trudeau dabbed at his forehead with a handkerchief.

"Sorry?"

"We're under attack and you are just standing there calmly. We're in earth orbit for pity's sake! Earth orbit and taking enemy fire."

"These are just drones...probably a few scattered flights which slipped past our scout patrols. No factory ship will get this close without being spotted."

"I wish that I shared your confidence." The Prime Minister turned back to studying the crew. "My nerves are shot."

"It's all right. Not everyone is cut out for combat." Arden offered a shrug. "I've been fighting for decades. I'm used to it by now."

"One carrier destroyed!"

A cheer went up.

"*Lao Hu* is firing on the second carrier. *Duan Gung* is shifting targets."

"Enemy drones are closing again."

"Where are my defensive batteries?" Franklin shouted. "By God, I'm going to start running snap drills for the next month!"

"I'm the Prime Minister of the United Human Worlds. I'm not supposed to ever be in a combat zone."

"I'll have a word with the Joint Chiefs about your safety."

"Do that."

"Last wave of drones closing!"

"Gun crews!" Franklin bellowed.

"One's getting through!"

"Suicide ship!"

"Good God!" Trudeau swore.

Freedom Station didn't even shudder.

"We're bigger than a ship." Arden was still quite calm. "There's no real danger."

Trudeau frowned at him.

* * *

"The retreat from Mars." Collin Zane shook his head and slumped against the restraints holding him in his chair. "I never thought to see the day."

"We'll regroup at LaGrange Four. Mars Colony is going to hold out."

"Of course, Kemp." Zane tried to keep his voice confident. "Admiral Jarrell still has most of his defense grid." His mobile battle fleet was all-but-shattered though. The battered remnants of First Fleet would never be able to hold out for long against a concerted enemy attack.

"First we lost Hunter's Moon, and now Mars."

"We haven't lost Mars, Boxleitner. We've just been cut off from our garrison there." *Hopefully not for long*, Zane thought grimly. "What is the latest word from Earth?"

Wolfgang checked his files. "The raids against the defence grid have slackened. General Franklin has been hailed as a hero for holding out and preventing any ground attack runs."

"Old Firestorm was never much for holding a line...he was always much happier on the offensive." Felix Boxleitner offered that comment with a touch of amusement in his voice. "He hammered the rebels during the Canal Wars."

"His campaign for the reduction of Cooke II is now required reading for all fleet officers," Zane agreed.

"I can't wait to read his report on these raids."

"Should be interesting," Zane agreed.

"Incoming transmission," Wolfgang reported. "It's from Admiral Jarrell. Text only."

"So he doesn't want to talk to me directly? What does he want?"

Wolfgang read the message over. "We're to regroup with the remains of Fourth Fleet and then take over escorting a freighter convoy to Earth orbit before they depart on their next mission."

"Transfer the coordinates to the helm and set a course." Zane took a deep breath. "Best speed, Jankowski."

"Aye, Captain."

* * *

"Your new orders, Admiral, are for you to relieve the garrison at Io Station."

Dale Arden looked coldly across the oak desk at Singh. "That garrison is beyond relief, Ashvim, and we both know it."

Singh turned his head slightly, the ghost of a smile playing across his lips. "Are you questioning the orders of the Sol System Commander?" he asked in a dangerously low tone.

Arden heard the danger, but ignored it. "Yes, I am." The office was small and minimally furnished. *Not what I would expect Singh to have...I expected him to be surrounded by momentoes of his past triumphs.*

"Nonetheless, you *will* proceed to Io or you will be relieved of your command."

"It's madness. We're wasting our ships on a mission like that."

"You have your orders...we cannot allow any more of our colonies to fall to these invaders."

"No matter the cost?"

Singh did not reply.

"Do I get access to any more ships?"

"You have to use what you have available. Dale, you of all people know just how much UHW Spacey's resources are stretched to the limit right now." Singh tried to put a sound of conciliation in his voice.

Arden frowned. "Then why waste ships attempting to relieve Io? We have to cut our losses and consolidate."

"Fall back to Earth?"

"That *is* the one world we cannot afford to lose."

"Earth is in no serious danger." The other member of the Joint Chiefs shook his head. "Our orbital defence grid is strong. Our local mobile forces stand ready to defend this world to their deaths."

"Are their deaths going to be matched with your own, Singh?"

"If Earth falls, I will fall in its defence."

"I'll hold you to that."

"Is that a threat?"

Arden merely smiled.

Chapter Eighteen

Boxleitner eyed the visuals of the battered fleet with a critical eye. "Not too much left of them." The fleet's remnants were maintaining a ragged formation, and not one that would likely do much good against a Devastator attack.

Zane shook his head and he handed a datapad to an aide. "They've had a fighting withdrawal from Tau Ceti. I'm not surpised that they took such heavy casualties."

"And they're still covering civilians?"

"Most of them are from Io and beyond." The civilians were retreating from Io and other outer colonies for the dubious protection of being on Earth. The freighters and other converted ships were not combatants and their battered and scorched hulls plainly showed the cost of battles they had survived. *I can't imagine what they must have gone through.* "Wolfgang, hail the fleet and offer our assistance."

"Aye, Sir."

Zane's small battle group was hardly worth the name, but it might help their morale at least. "Jankowski, plot a course for LaGrange Three. We'll head there first."

"Aye, Captain."

"Regroup at the habitats?"

"It's the best place right now."

* * *

"The *Barghest* is taking fire!"

"Damn it!" Arden shook his head as the display screen lit up with drone icons. "Where the hell did they call come from?" he demanded as a fresh wave of drones swarmed around the *Deliverance*.

"Too many ships." Marcus Chapman shook his own head. "Admiral, I don't think we can retake Io Station."

"There's not much left to retake."

Half of the ring-shaped Io Station was simply *gone* and a massive factory ship hovered nearby. Surge cannons on the Station were still firing intermittently, striking at the factory ship.

"The *Beowulf* is breaking formation."

"Order it back into position."

"No response."

Arden cursed.

"Get me a firing solution on that carrier," Chapman called out.

"Locked."

"Fire at will!"

"Detecting civilian traffic."

"Civilians?" What the hell were they doing out here?"

"*Garm* is moving into firing position."

"I want a targeting solution on the second carrier. Full missile spread."

"Yes, Admiral." Chapman snapped a string of orders to his crew. "And the factory ship?"

"First we clear away its escorts," Arden said, "and then we'll see about dealing with that factory ship."

"Missile racks loaded and armed. Carrier is coming about."

"Fire at will."

"Drones on intercept!"

"Surge cannons to defensive fire!" Chapman ordered. "Fire all batteries as they pass."

"Damage control teams are standing by."

"*Grendal* is hurt...hull breaches on all decks."

"Can we give any cover fire?"

"No, Sir. They're too far out of formation."

"Damn it!" Arden slammed his fist onto the arm of his chair. "We have to do something."

"But what?"

"That is the question." *I knew this wouldn't work. I warned Singh!* Dale felt the *Eye of Ra* shake.

* * *

"Approaching LaGrange Three."

"Take us in, and slow to a safe speed." The visual display was impressive. Zane could see dozens of cylindrical habitats on the main screen. They were rotating and lights blinked across their hulls. Shuttles and small civilian ships slipped between the the large stations. "Request the docking assignments from Liberty Station." He didn't see many warships in the area though. *I only see two or three* Deliverances. *Where did they all go? Why is LaGrange Three undefended?*

"Transmitting clearance codes now."

"Any report of Devastator activity in the area?"

"Negative on that, Captain." Boxleitner shook his head. "It's been pretty quiet in the inner system." He paused. "The big battle is out near Io. And Mars. Just minor raiding actions around here."

"For now.'"

"Yeah, for now."

"Captain, we're receiving a data-stream...landing assignments for the civilians."

"Good." Zane leaned back in his chair. "Transfer instructions to the various ship captains so they can dock. Have the civilians off-loaded as quickly as can be arranged." He could only imagine how cramped those evacuation ships actually had to be. *At least there is plenty of room in that collection of habitats for them.*

"The civilians should be safe here."

"As safe as can be arranged," Zane agreed. Most of the LaGrange habitats had their own defensive weaponry, which should be sufficient to fend off drones and carriers. A few of the stations were dedicated military installions with even heavier firepower. *And since the invasion, a number of OWPs have been built out here as well.* The habitats were prepared and capable of defending themselves. *I hope*. Against a factory ship however...but then if a factory ship came this close, the habitats were truly doomed.

"Captain, your presence is being requested by Liberty Station."

"My presence, Wolfgang?"

"Aye, Sir. And they're asking for you to bring along Commander Boxleitner as well."

Felix turned his head away from his console with a frown on his rugged face. "Why do they want me?"

"Why do they want either of us?" Zane considered the request and then he shrugged. "Acknowledge the request. We'll be arranging to shuttle over shortly."

"Yes, Captain."

"Be nice to at least get back into some decent gravity," Boxleitner said after a moment.

"Even if it's not real," Zane agreed. "On that note, arrange for the crew to have some leave over on *Liberty*. It will do them good."

"For once we don't need to keep the crew on damage repair."

"No, we don't." The *Hellstorm* was in fine condition for a change.

"I'll have our supply requisition ready to transmit shortly."

"Send it when you're done." Zane unfastened his chair restraints and propeled himself across the bridge. "Come along, Commander. Let's get to that shuttle and find out who want us."

The station's hanger doors closed even as the sleek shuttle was settling onto its landing pad. Air was quickly pumped back in and the hanger bay repressurized quickly.

Zane and Boxleitner stepped through the inner hatch, ignoring the grey-uniformed technicians who were now hurrying acoss the deck to refuel the shuttle.

"I miss gravity." Boxleitner stretched out his back. "Even the artifical stuff." The hanger bay was cold though.

"Some day we'll develope the technology to have gravity on our ships." Zane was confident of it. "Or at least build ships with sections we can rotate to simulate gravity."

"That would be impractical on a warship," Boxleitner replied with a snort. "One solid hit and the grav deck would be smashed. Just be a big target on a lumbering warship."

"Perhaps."

A man in a grey uniform was approaching, with a determined looked on his face. "Captain. Commander." His dark hair was cropped extremely short and a nasty-looking scar crossed his left cheek.

"Corporal."

The officer saluted. "Corporal Damian Bowie. You are both expected in the deckmaster's office. Sirs."

Why there? Zane frowned. "Very well. Lead the way." He gave his jacket another tug to adjust it. *Something we don't have to do in zero-gee,* he thought in amusement.

The hatch hissed open.

Zane stepped into the small office. "Collin Zane, Captain of the *Hellstorm*, reporting as ordered," he said before even finishing his entrance with Felix at his heels.

"Hello, Zane."

Zane stared. "Kathleen."

Kathleen Levy smiled at him with amusement from where she stood beside the small desk. She was wearing the businesslike dark green skirt and vest, with a fiery red blouse, that Zane was used to seeing her often wearing around the Government Complex.

"What are you doing here?"

"What, no hello?" Kathleen took a step towards him. "I thought that you might at least have missed me a little."

"Of course I missed you." Zane wasn't sure exactly what to say. "What the hell are you doing out here? You should be safe back on Earth."

"No place is safe in this war, Zane. An UHW Spacey officer should know that."

"Earth is a damn bit safer than being on a colony."

"True, but Parliament required a representative out here...and I was chosen to be the lucky one. Departmental politics and the like." She shrugged, and then brushed a hand through her hair. "And this must be the famous Commander Boxleitner."

"You know my executive officer?"

"Only by reputation and rumour." As she said that, Kathleen turned and walked back over to the small desk. "You can come in now," she said into the intercom. She turned back towards Zane. "I was quite happy to find out that you were escorting the civilians here."

"And why is that?"

"Because then I could see you again." Kathleen took several steps towards him with an even wider smile on her face. "And so I could see this...."

The door hissed open.

"Felix?"

Boxleitner's face was white. He stared at the figure in the open doorway, his mouth moving but no sounds emerged.

Zane stared. "What the—"

"Felix, it's me." The red-haired woman stepped fully into the office.

"Anna?" Felix ran across the room and grabbed his wife in his arms. "Anna, you're alive!" There were tears in his eyes. "My God, you're alive."

She pressed her face into his chest.

Zane blinked his own eyes to clear them, and then turned his head to the beaming politician. "How did you—"

Kathleen brushed at her own eyes. "Just enjoy the moment," she said.

* * *

"We're being recalled to battle."

Zane nodded at his executive officer. "Yes, we are." He then twisted his head to look over at Kathleen with a sad twist to his mouth. Three weeks had gone by all too quickly for his taste. "All too quickly." The restaurant was noisy and he was enjoying being just another face in the crowd. *I'm not in charge here. I'm not the captain.* It made for a refreshing change. Neither he nor Boxleitner was wearing his uniform. *Kathleen told us to dress casual for tonight.*

"I could pull some strings," Kathleen suggested. She was wearing a stunning jade-green gown, with an extremely low-cut neckline. "I could try to pull some strings and get the *Hellstorm* assigned to patrol the LaGrange point colonies."

"No, I don't want special treatment."

"Neither do I," Felix Boxleitner agreed. "We're at war. We have to go wherever we're needed. We have to do whatever it takes to survive. The United Human Worlds needs that commitment from every officer."

Anna Boxleitner took another swallow from her wine glass and said nothing.

"You survived a lot, Anna." Zane reached for his own wine glass. "Felix was certain that you'd been killed at *Masada*."

"I'm sorry for the lack of contact." She paused a moment. "Like I explained earlier, the *Icarus* was crippled in the attack. We were trying to reach the wormhole and escape when the Devastators opened fire on *Masada*. When the wormhole collapsed, the backlash tossed us away. It took us days just to get the ship's engines back online and regain control. We were tumbling helplessly. Then we had to figure out where we were and plot a course back to the inhabited portions of the system. With our comm-system fried and so many systems damaged, it was harder than expected."

"A science ship in the Sol System and it was virtually lost." Kathleen shook her head. "Being cut off like that is almost unthinkable."

"It happened. A freak accident. We should have been killed." Anna patted Felix's knee. "We were thrown so far from the nadir point that it made the most sense for us to come here, to LaGrange Three, after regaining thrusters. Our resources were strained...we could only repair a handful of the crippled systems and the comm was completely useless."

"It's going to have to be replaced completely," Kathleen added. "The *Icarus* is most likely going to be spending a long time in the repair yards. The damage is pretty extensive."

"And yard space is limited right now."

Zane heard the irritation in her voice. "At least you survived."

"Yes, I was one of the lucky ones." Anna looked down at the tabletop. "Doctor Wasser wasn't. Neither was Chiang."

Felix winced.

Zane refilled their wine glasses.

One waiter took their empty plates away and another hurriedly brought a tray of assorted pastries and fruit.

"Oranges." Felix snatched for one of the round oranges with unseemly haste. Then he gasped and winced. "I love fresh oranges," he apologized as he reached under the table with his right hand.

Anna gave him a too-sweet smile. "Someday I'll teach him table manners."

Zane and Levy grinned at each other.

"So is the *Marco Polo* repairable?"

"Yes, but OPE doesn't know when they'll be able to launch another expedition to Alpha Omega. Too much traffic out-system is made of people evacuating for safer colonies. If any such exist."

"In the meantime, Doctor Boxleitner has accepted a position on my staff." Levy looked back at Zane, matching him look-for-look. "What?"

"Why do you need a xeno-archeologist?"

"UHW Spacey R&D has been studying Devastator technology for some time. OPE has been studying alien technologies as well. Non-Ospma ones I mean." Whatever they could dig up on dead worlds. "Liberty Station was the sight of humanity's first contact with the Ospma. We've uncovered some new vid-recordings and data from that time."

"Lost in an old section of the station where no one has gone in decades." Anna laughed. "Here I was getting ready to head hundreds of lightyears away towards the rim, and there's an archeological mystery right here at home."

"Hence the reason Parliament sent you out here?"

"Yep." Kathleen nodded. "I told Beth you could be clever."

Zane blushed as Felix chuckled.

"We have also obtained some samples of Devastator technology that I'd like to have examined."

"But Anna isn't that kind of scientist."

"No, but we've got plenty of *that kind* of scientists...I want someone fresh to look at it. She might see something no one else has."

"Kathleen hopes that I'll think outside the box."

"It's possible."

"In terms of Devastator technologies, I don't even know that there is a box." Anna laughed. "So I guess I'll be perfect for the job."

"Good luck with that," Zane reached for his wine.

* * *

"Factory ship is launching more drones."

"Continue firing!"

Dale Arden heard the anger in Captain Chapman's voice. *Tempers are running hot since the failure to retake Io Station.* The Fourth Fleet had been hammered before the order to retreat, but UHW Spacey had hurt the Devastators just as badly in the process. *We lost half our battle fleet...but they lost just as many ships.* Two factory ships were now little more than expanding clouds of half-melted scrap...that had to be counted as a victory. *We must have hurt them...they've sent another factory ship and its escorts after us.*

"Captain, the constant rate of fire is diverting energy away from our engines."

"I know that, Davis."

"Incoming drones...interceptors running hot."

"ECM is not jamming their controls."

"Increase power, Juegan."

"*Ymir* is firing on a carrier...multiple missiles closing fast."

"Scratch one carrier!"

"*Stormcrow* reports critical engine damage."

"Understood, Ortega. Juegan, what's in position to support that freighter?"

"Nothing, Admiral."

Arden winced at Juegan's harsh honesty. *We're supposed to be protecting the civilians, not watching them die.* His gaze flicked to a display. *Crew of thirty, estimating four hundred and nineteen civilians.*

"*Bifrost* is slowing, altering its course to cover the *Stormcrow*."

"Order the *Bifrost* to maintain current course and speed." Arden hated himself for giving that order. "We can't afford to slow the convoy down for anything."

Chapman looked at him.

"Maintain course and speed. The convoy does not stop for any reason." Not until they could rendezvous with other UHW Spacey units. *There must be some nearby. There has to be!* "Any word on that Ospma patrol?"

"No, Admiral. I've been unable to establish contact."

"I hope they didn't run into a Devastator patrol."

"So do I, Captain."

"We're being targeted by multiple units!"

The *Deliverance*-class cruiser lurched as turbo-charged lasers punched through its aft section.

A console exploded as its power systems overloaded, then a second followed.

The ceiling lights failed, plunging the bridge into darkness broken by flickering displays and burning consoles.

Two crewmen hurried over with fire extinguishers.

"Damage report!" Arden shouted over the wail of alarms when Captain Chapman remained silent. *Where is he?* The bridge was hazy with smoke and the light panels were dark.

"Aft hull breached...main engines off-line."

"Weapon systems off-line!"

"Internal power web is overloaded."

"Restore power! Where is Chapman?" Arden looked around the dimly lit bridge. The flickering lights and showers of sparks made it a scene from some nightmare. "What's our status, Davis?"

"Attempting to regain control." The helmsman hammered at his controls. "Engines are dead."

"Reactor status?"

"Singularity is holding steady."

"Thank God for small favours." The singularity wasn't likely to consume the ship anytime soon then. "Ortega, order the convoy to run! Leave us behind."

"Admiral?"

"Run...we're expendable." There were civilians on those ships and they had to be protected. "The convoy slows for no one!"

"Yes, Sir."

"Enemy carriers breaking off!" Juegan sounded shocked.

"Why?"

"Another ship has arrived...it's the *Hellstorm*!"

Arden took a breath, and coughed as he inhaled some of the acrid smoke. "Order Captain Zane to guard the civilians as they retreat."

"Aye, Admiral."

"Transfer all remaining power reserves to the weapon batteries. Hit the drones with everything you can muster. Distract the Devastators, draw them into attacking us." It was all that he could do now. "Give the others a chance to escape."

"Energy spike!" Juegan called out. "Wormhole opening!"

With a blinding flash, an energy whirlpool swirled open. By chance, or design, the vortex clipped the factory ship.

Arden winced as the huge factory ship tore itself apart in a fiery series of explosions.

"What the hell just happened?" Juegan gasped.

"Reinforcements."

"Not ours." UHW Spacey could never have opened a vortex so successfully. "Are they Ospma?"

"Negative. Admiral, they're broadcasting with Raptchi identification beacons!" Ortega shook his head in disbelief.

Zane stared at the display. "What the hell are those things?" he asked as a dozen ships emerged from the wormhole before it imploded behind them.

"I have no idea." Boxleitner checked the sensors and studied one of the unfamiliar ship silhouettes. "They're throwing out a lot of firepower though."

The largest warship—its hull painted a dark green with red striping—unleashed a barrage of energy bolts which erupted against a blocky carrier. Two of the smaller designs vaporized a flight of drones with energy bursts.

"They're very good."

"Against the Devastators, they'll need to be."

"Then let's not let ourselves be shown up." Zane cleared his throat. "Alter course for that carrier." He designated a target. "All batteries, fire at will."

The last carrier exploded.

"Only a handful of drones are still flying," Juegan reported. "The Raptchi are moving to intercept." Drones did not retreat of course—they would continue to attack until they either drained their power reserves or else were destroyed.

"Good to hear. Order the convoy to reform." Arden shook his head to clear his thoughts. "Such as it is." *So many lives lost,* he thought bitterly. The convoy was composed of all the ships left from Fourth Fleet. *They barely make up a task force now,* he thought to himself. *And their admiral was lost along with his flagship.* It had been a bitter defeat at Io, despite his claims to the contrary.

"We're being hailed by the Raptchi flagship."

"Let me hear it, Ortega."

"*This is Las'li-drac. Care to come aboard, Admiral Arden?*"

He heard the amusement clearly in her voice. "Yes, I would, WarMaster."

Chapter Nineteen

"The loss of Mars will cripple us." Lee Hwan Kim shook his head slowly. The mug sitting on the table in front of him was untouched. "Trying to keep the full extent of the defeat there from the media is extremely difficult. They are going to find out and it's going to set off riots."

Vanya Ivanova grimaced. "We haven't *lost* Mars...we've just been cut off from our garrison there."

"Admiral Jarrell has failed. He should be stripped of his—"

"He's dead, Romano." Ashvim Singh leaned over the table, managing to look upset by the news he delivered to the assembled members of the Joint Chiefs. "A small loss. I will now have to assume overall command over the defence of the Sol System."

The other admirals and Joint Chiefs were silent. Prime Minister Trudeau remained sitting silently in his own chair.

Singh knew that they would be shock for a while—and that would be his time to move. "With Mars cut off, we need to reexamine our deployments for the Outer System Colonies."

"Io?" Kim looked up from the table.

"Yes, the Io Transfer Point does require reinforcement."

"Fourth Fleet is operating in that area."

"Fourth Fleet is currently more fiction than fact, Jennifer." Singh gestured as General Romano studied an updated display. "Admiral Marc Gascoigne has been all but wiped out at Tau Ceti. The handful of ships that actually responded to our recall signal will probably not even manage to slow down a serious Devastator attack. Assuming that Arden survives long enough to take command of them. I have my doubts in our colleague's abilities of late."

"The Fourth was shattered at Tau Ceti, but they're still ready and willing to fight. Gascoigne went after the factory fleet at Io—"

"And were all-but-destroyed."

"They covered the evacuation of the civilians away from there," Ivanova argued. "Thousands of them are en route to Earth."

"So they can die here?"

Singh turned his head. "You said something, Romano?"

"No." The general shook her head. "Nothing."

"They are brave," Kim argued. "Admiral Arden has taken command of that fleet. He will no doubt execute a delaying fight to slow the Devastators."

If he survives, Singh thought after Kim had fallen silent. "Which is more than can be said for Admiral Kopinski. You have some current news of him, Admiral Kim?"

The Director of Military Intelligence shook his head. "There has been no further contact with any elements assigned to Sixth Fleet. A scouting party has transited into Kapteyn...the naval base is gone."

Gone. The word hung in the air.

"We've lost almost all of our colonies."

Every eye turned towards the Prime Minister. He looked back at them, matching their surprise with a calmness and serenity of his own. *Did you all forget that I was here?* Trudeau wondered. "We have almost nothing left. At this rate, the Human race will be extinct by year's end."

"That is not a helpful attitude."

"I know that, Romano."

Jennifer blinked at his tone.

"We must be realists." Trudeau looked hard at his staff. "The fate and survival of the Human race depends upon the choices we are making. We must find a means of winning this war."

Singh nodded his head in silent agreement.

* * *

Collin Zane looked around the hanger bay. "I'm still not sure I like the idea of this, Admiral." His breath was visible—the hanger was still cold despite the efforts of the ship's life support systems.

"I'll be fine, Captain." Dale Arden tilted his head to one side and chuckled.

Felix Boxleitner was standing just behind them, also wearing a pistol. "We're just concerned for your safety."

Arden was still chuckling. "It is a bit late to change your mind about coming over here with me." The small *Eagle*-class shuttle was already resting on the deckplates of the Raptchi flagship after all. "If the Raptchi were hostile, I think we'd already be dead."

"I know that, Sir." Collin Zane shook his head, and then quickly checked his holstered sidearm. He glanced around the hanger bay one more time, but saw nothing out of the ordinary. "Her arrival seems just too coincidental."

"And here I thought that your Earther culture appreciated the calvary galloping over a hill in the proverbial nick of time?"

At that mocking voice, Arden turned his head towards the distant hatch with an amused smile on his face. "WarMaster Las'li-drac."

She nodded her head to him. "Admiral Arden." Two black-uniformed soldiers stood at her back. "Our sensors noted that you had brought guests with you this time."

"Captain Zane Zane and his first officer, Commander Felix Boxleitner."

She strode forward, away from her guards, her boots clicking loudly on the deckplates. She held out her hand in the Human manner of greeting. "Ah, the famous Commander Boxleitner."

"Famous?" he asked in surprise.

"You destroyed a Silencer factory ship...never a simple task."

"You took one out," he countered.

"With our arrival? Purely luck."

"I don't believe in luck."

"No, you believe in superior firepower." Las'li-drac smiled more widely, baring her pointed teeth. "I like that." She gestured. "Come, let us retire to a place where we can talk in some comfort."

The hatch hissed closed with a distinctive *clunk* as it sealed.

Zane eyed the room—it was apparently the WarMaster's personal quarters. The bulkheads were the same colouring as the rest of the ship's corridors, but here a few pieces of artwork hung on them. "Your fleet handled itself well in that engagement. I didn't see many wasted shots."

Boxleitner nodded. "On the contrary, your fleet attacked with a unity of purpose that I've rarely seen."

They attacked the Devastators like a pack of starving wolves going after a lame deer, Zane thought.

"We've had considerable experience with the Silencers." Las'li-drac gestured to a bottle and glasses on a low table. "Shall we split a bottle of *driskata* to celebrate our little victory?" She poured out four glasses of the pale green liquid.

Arden accepted his glass. "Yes, I suppose we should."

Zane eyed the liquid. "Is it safe?" he asked. "It smells...powerful." From the strong smell, he wondered if it would melt through hull armour.

"She didn't poison me the last time we met."

"You've been meeting with her?"

Arden looked back at the UHW Spacey captain with a calm expression on his face. "Is there some reason I should not have been?"

Boxleitner licked his lips. "I haven't heard anything on the news nets about negotiations with non-Ospma. I would have thought that—"

"The Ospma think quite highly of themselves." The Raptchi fleet officer chuckled and sat down in a chair. "I don't see them holding off the Silencers though."

"No, but our combined forces—"

"Yes, Captain Zane, your combined forces have been fighting for centuries." Las'li-drac allowed a hint of mockery to colour her voice. "Have you studied star charts?"

He frowned at the question. "Of course."

"Have you ever studied star charts *not* supplied by the Ospma?" Her eyes narrowed, and her lips parted in amusement. "They can make for very entertaining reading."

"What are you hinting at?"

The Raptchi turned to look at Dale Arden with her still-narrowed eyes. "Since the Ospma first encouraged your race to spread out and colonize new territory, there has been a shift in military operations. The bulk of recorded Devastator attacks have been made against United Human Worlds holdings."

Arden shook his head. "But the Goolatch—"

"Lost heavily yes, as did other races who were unfortunate enough to be in the line of fire. However, from what I have observed, the Ospma have managed to lure the bulk of Silencer factory ships spinward." She sipped at her drink. "Into the United Human Worlds."

Boxleitner shook his head. His glass of *driskata* was still untouched. "You're claiming that our allies have sold us out?"

"I have scouting reports which show three Ospma worlds lost to the Silencers in the last twenty years." She tilted her head to the left. "How many worlds have you lost in the same period?"

"Too many." Arden finished his *driskata*. "Far too many."

"The Ospma have lost worlds too," Zane argued. "Seventh Fleet has been fighting there for years. They've seen Baronies fall."

"Minor colonies and outposts only. A handful of sacrifices to allay any suspicions you might have."

"Those are incredible claims, Las'li-drac."

"I have datafiles if you wish to view them, Arden."

He said nothing.

Would we trust those files of yours? "So why are you here?" Zane demanded. "Why come to Earth?"

"To save you from destruction?" Her cat-like eyes gleamed. "Your people have much potential for greatness. I hope be able to channel some of that into battle on our behalf." She refilled her glass, and then poured more *driskata* for Arden.

"You want allies."

"Don't you?"

Arden took a sip from his refilled glass. "Is your Imperium prepared to supply military aid to Earth?"

"Officially? *No.*" She was still smiling. "However, the WarMasters have not yet taken a formal vote on the subject of aiding the United Human Worlds, and so we have plenty of *unofficial* room in which we can maneuver."

"I don't understand."

"Once the Council votes on a matter, then discussion is closed and everyone supports that decision without hesitation or holding back. As there has been neither vote nor decision, I am free to commit my personal forces however I see fit. By fighting here, we can distract the Silencers from exploring more space and seeking out the holdings of my people's Imperium. Destroying them here, saves my people."

"And if you die here?"

"Then I die along with my command. No risk, no glory."

"I see." Arden rubbed at his chin.

"Overall I have been most entertained by watching your struggle. A most innovative tactic, Commander Boxleitner, on your part."

"Thank you. I think."

"Deploying nuclear warheads from your hanger bay...letting the Silencers pull the missiles onboard with their own tractor beams. Brilliant! You slipped the nukes right past their deflector screens. Brilliant, I say!"

"How do you know about that?"

"I watched the news." She laughed again. "No wonder the Ospma thought that Humans would make wonderful allies. It will be a pleasure fighting with you."

I have never heard an Ospma laugh, Arden thought.

* * *

"Where the hell were your people?"

Gorpshan settled himself on the floor of the office. As usual, the Ospma did not bother to attempt to sit in one of the Human-style chairs, but chose to remain on the carpet.

"Earth is in a crisis right now." The office was empty, aside from Trudeau and Gorpshan. The Prime Minister's dark suit was rumpled and he had thrown aside his tie earlier in the day. He was standing with his back to the window overlooking the Green Well.

"The galaxy is in crisis." The Ospma's mouthparts rubbed together. "The war proceeds as it has done. With the Prime Devastator lurking somewhere in the Sol System, it becomes a target. Skirmishes continue and the war—"

"The war is being lost!" Trudeau snapped at him loudly. "Don't you understand that?"

Lilac and mauve patterns rippled across Gorpshan's leathery skin. "UHW Spacey remains strong."

"Not strong enough." Trudeau took a deep breath, inhaling the salty scent of the Ospma. "For centuries, we've been fighting the Devastators, defending the United Human Worlds *and* the Baronies. Despite our best efforts, we've failed to hold and star system after star system has fallen. We have only a handful of colonies left to us!

"We need more physical support from the Baronies. The Joint Chiefs are demanding it. Parliament is demanding it. Hell, *I* am demanding it."

A dozen of Gorpshan's eyes blinked slowly.

"UHW Spacey is virtually shattered. We have almost nothing left to throw into battle."

"The Baronies rely on you for strength." Gorpshan rasped that out. His tentacle-arms waved.

"We have spent our strength. Gorpshan, we need *allies*. The conference you hosted last year provoked talk. We need to build on that dialogue."

"Talks fail. Military strength understood."

"We cannot stand alone."

"Io Station has fallen."

"Yes, it has," Trudeau agreed. "Fourth Fleet is all but destroyed—its remnants are fleeing to the LaGrange Habitats. Sixth Fleet is simply *gone*. I don't hold out much hope for any of the other fleets we have scattered around the galaxy. The United Human Worlds is dying and I don't want to admit it, but I might very well be the last prime minister."

"There has been interference."

Trudeau frowned.

Gorpshan raised a tentacle-arm and curled it into an intricate gesture. "Outsiders have violated the Sol System."

"Outsiders?" Trudeau blinked at the comment. "I am not aware of any new fleets operating within the United Human Worlds. Have allies come to our aid?"

"An Essan scout detected a wormhole vortex. Contact was lost with the scout before a full report could be made."

"More Devastators?"

The Ospma did not reply.

"I can't see anyone attacking one of your scouts," Trudeau argued. "Human or supposed ally. Where was this ship located?"

"Uncertain."

"I see." Trudeau frowned. "Tell me more about this signal."

"Alien. Vortex opened. Ship emerged."

"Transfer whatever hard data you have to my office. I'll have the matter investigated."

"Essan are checking."

"I would like to run my own analysis, Gorpshan."

The Ospma said nothing.

"You want me to divert ships to patrol, when I need every warship defending our colonies. You have to give me something to work with."

"More Essan come. The intruders will be destroyed." Gorpshan began undulating his way across the carpet.

Not even a good-bye? Trudeau was long since used to the Ospma's lack of Human-style manners. *It's going to take hours to get ride of that smell.* He triggered the office's ventilation system.

* * *

"We have received several communiqués from Admiral Arden's ship.'" The black uniformed Raptchi offered a crisp salute. "Their Fourth Fleet is being ordered to gather at LaGrange Three for repair and resupply."

"Thank you, Des'ran."

"Enemy units are continuing to mass at several staging points."

"Are those the latest reports?" Arden accepted the comp-pad and glanced at its small display. It was the same basic design as the Human ones he was used too, though it felt lighter despite being the same size. "I see."

Las'li-drac frowned as she glanced at the bridge's main display screen. "The Ospma deign to supply you with scouting reports at least. One can only hope that they are accurate."

"They fight as well." Arden raised his head and looked around. The command deck was more spacious than any Human vessel...larger than on some space stations. The artificial gravity felt nice too.

"Not recently, from what I have observed."

"They were present during the recent battle at *Masada.*"

"Your people fought brilliantly there," Las'li-drac told him. "I do not see how they could have fought differently. The Silencers were too numerous and too powerful to be held off."

"If they are too numerous and too powerful when they hit *Masada,* then how can we hope to keep them away from Earth?"

"That is a strategy we must discover." Displays flickered as they were updated with new data.

Arden looked at the Raptchi aide. "Any new information from the Joint Chiefs?"

"No, Admiral." Des'ran gave the Human the exact same amount of respect he gave to his own WarMaster. "The message traffic has been sparse of late."

Arden frowned. "I don't like this enforced silence." He lifted his eyes away from the comp-pad. "Las'li-drac, can you spare some ships to transit out of the system?"

A faint look of interest flashed across her face. "You want to conduct a reconnaissance raid?"

"I want you to send a ship to Orion Seven. Admiral Hague should be there, at the naval base. I'll be sending a data crystal with orders for him to divert a portion of Fifth Fleet to support us."

"I'll have a ship prepped for immediate transit." Las'li-drac gestured to another aide who had previously approached. "But I must admit that fuel reserves could be a problem."

"The garrison at Orion can restock you."

"Assuming that this garrison still exists. Oh, don't worry for I will send a ship there, but I merely point out that many of your United Human Worlds colonies have gone quiet. I do not know if it is from their destruction or because they wish to hide and hope the Silencers do not stumble across them."

"The United Human Worlds are dying," Arden agreed in a grim tone of voice. "Despite our best efforts to the contrary."

"The Ospma have done your people no favours in bringing you out into the greater galaxy."

"They gave us the stars, Las'li-drac, and that was a worthwhile prize."

"Which will now cost your people everything."

"The Silencers would have found us eventually. That is what everyone tends to think. They're sweeping across space, one system at a time. At least this way we had multiple battle fleets ready to fight and delay them."

"A good way to look at things." She gave him a studying look. "With better technology, you might have stood more of a chance."

"The Silencers are too powerful."

"No, the Ospma have hobbled you. There are other races with such advanced-to-you technology. Why don't you have worm-engines on more of your ships?"

"The components are too rare."

"Quantium-forty is rare, but not impossible to find. The Ospma don't have a monopoly on every secret in the galaxy. They limited you with an engineered scarcity of worm-engines and made you reliant upon these transit-stations. *Masada* and *Leonidas* tied you down. Limited your ability to move ships freely about the galaxy."

"They provide protection."

"Only a limited amount. They certainly don't stop me from coming and going." She laughed at his look of annoyance.

"So what other choice is there?"

"Find non-Ospma sources of technology."

"We have explorers and xeno-archeologists doing just that." Not that any of the expeditions had been successful recently. "I know that Admiral Webber's research and development teams have been trying to replicate the Silencers' own faster than light propulsion system."

"Oh?"

"But they've had no luck so far. Their carriers tend to be wrecked in battles, blown up beyond worthwhile salvaging."

"We've found the same."

"And the factory ships are virtually impossible to capture intact. By the time we batter one into immobility, it's usually become a cloud of debris."

"Very true." Las'li-drac half-closed her yellow eyes. "Their technology is extremely advanced in some ways and primitive in others. That gives us some advantage."

"But enough of one?"

Chapter Twenty

An alarm sounded.

"What is it?" Collin Zane demanded as he flung himself through the hatch and onto the *Hellstorm's* bridge. His eyes flicked across the bridge, hurriedly studying the displays.

"The sensor net has picked up an incoming Devastator task force," Wolfgang reported. "One factory ship, several carriers."

Zane spared a brief thought for the hundreds of thousands of civilians on the habitats even as he gripped the edge of a console. *Immobile targets for those Devastators to rip apart,* he thought as a cold chill scuttled along his back. "Order all warships to form up and prepare for battle." He pushed himself towards his chair.

Felix Boxleitner was already strapped into his chair. He looked tired, but eager. "I have a unit strength comparison ready."

"I don't want to know." UHW Spacey would be badly outnumbered. *We always are,* Zane thought grimly, *but we're going to put up one hell of a fight anyway.* "Have the habitats power up their defensive batteries." *No point in making this any easier for the Devastators than we have too.*

"We've sent a distress signal to Earth."

"For all the good it will do." Zane doubted UHW Spacey would divert any other ships away from Earth orbit. *Even if they do, reinforcements won't possibly be able to arrive in time.* "Any idea where Admiral Arden is?"

"No, Sir. He's still with Las'li-drac and the Raptchi are off on a patrol run of their own devising. Some unspecified form of combat maneuvers."

"Pity. He's going to miss quite a battle."

Boxleitner frowned at his monitor. "They always are."

Wolfgang cleared his throat. "Captain, we have contact with the Ospma."

"There's an Ospma flotilla here?"

"Aye, Captain." Wolfgang sounded as surprised as Zane did.

"How many ships?"

"One *Warsphere*, two *Battleglobes*, three *Resohexs*."

"Well, that's some good news at least." Zane took a deep breath. "I am assuming command of the defense. Order all ships to form up around us."

"That factory ship is the key."

"I know." Zane nodded to his exec. "And the Devastators are well aware of that fact as well."

"We have to engage them." Felix Boxleitner turned back to his console. "There are too many civilians in the area." His hand clenched into fists. *Anna is out there.* She was on Liberty Station.

"The habitats are heavily defended." The habitats were equipped with numerous surge cannons, and there were several military stations amongst them with missile racks and laser cannon.

"They won't be enough to hold off the Devastators! You know that. Sir."

"I do." Zane paused for a moment, and his exec looked ashamed by his outburst. "We will fight to defend the colonies. And," he added in a louder tone, "we will win. We have no other choice."

"Lead elements, open fire!" Zane was actually relieved once combat began. *Waiting for hours while the enemy fleet closes in is far more nerve-wracking then the actual battle.* He watched the bridge displays as the missiles launched. "Second squadron, go!"

Ospma *Battleglobes* accelerated to their full speed and swept past the carriers on a flanking maneuver the UHW Spacey ships could never hope to match.

Better manipulation of their power curves, Zane thought, *and an alien physiology rendering them able to tolerate higher gees than us.*

"Drones launching from the carriers."

"Stand by to engage."

"First Squadron is reporting good hits on their targets. Two carriers destroyed."

"Hopefully before they could launch," Boxleitner said in a low tone. "I hope the *Ymir* is ready." That particular *Deliverance* was charged with guarding the two *Torrential*-class cruisers against the incoming drones. The cruisers were best used for long-range attacks; with limited short-range guns, the drones would cut them to pieces.

"They're shifting their targeting systems."

"Firing main batteries."

"OWPs online and targeting now."

"And now the fun begins." Boxleitner managed to sound amused.

"Drones closing!" Kemp warned.

"Point defense teams are cleared to fire!"

"OWPs firing."

"Effect?"

"Lasers ineffectual due to their shielding. Missile hits on the carriers. Looks like solid hits...yes! One carrier destroyed."

"Continue the attack."

The *Battleglobes* soared past the factory ship, pelting it with bolts from their surge cannons.

"The Devastator carriers and drones are entering range of the habitats."

"Intensify all fire!" Zane shouted.

"Liberty Station is opening fire!"

Missiles began launching from the large station, accompanied by powerful bolts from its array of surge cannons.

Dozens of drones exploded.

"We're hitting them!"

"They're taking the hits deliberately." Boxleitner cursed loudly. "Those drones are shielding the carriers."

"Not for long." Zane smiled as the platform shifted its targeting and fired a massive volley at one single carrier. There were not enough drones in position to intercept and most of the missiles struck in bright explosions.

"Carrier destroyed."

"If only factory ships died that easily." Zane watched as a second weapon platform fired a few volleys of light missiles, to wear away the swarming drones, before switching to a volley of ship-killers. "How are the other Ospma doing?"

"They're still engaged. The factory ship is firing back, but so far no solid hits."

"Good."

"Captain, habitat Aldrin-Sixteen is reporting hull breaches." Wolfgang cursed softly. "Drones are swarming it. Its surge cannons are overheating."

"What's close to support them?"

"Nothing."

The *Hellstorm* shuddered.

Zane felt his restraints dig into his skin. *That's gonna leave a bruise,* he thought in annoyance. "Report!"

"Minor damage to forward hull."

"Drones are swarming our *Endor*."

"Trying to cut its jamming...we must be having some effect. Give them more cover fire! If we lose the jamming...."

"I know, I know!" Kemp snapped orders to his gunners.

"The factory ship is continuing forward," Wolfgang warned.

Boxleitner swallowed in a suddenly dry throat. "If that ship reaches a habitat...."

"I know, I know!" Zane winced. *How many new carriers could it manufacture from a habitat? How many thousands of drones? How many dead civilians?* "Third Squadron is cleared to engage." He was calling in his reserves, but what choice did he have?

"Factory ship closing on Aldrin-Three."

The stately spin of one of the cylindrical habitats faltered as green turbocharged laser bolts vapourized tons of hull plating.

"Fire all batteries!" Zane shouted. "Order remaining support ships to engage. That factory ship is our primary target."

The *Warsphere* hammered a carrier with repeated volleys from its array of surge cannon.

The carrier's deflector screens flared with light as the electro-magnetic bolts splashed against it.

Two *Torrential*-class cruisers fired missiles into the carrier as its shields failed and the blocky carrier exploded.

"Drones engaging the habitats."

Blue energy bolts flashed from the factory ship.

"The *Warsphere* is unaffected."

"Yes, the Ospma are particularly immune to that electrical disruption weapon." It was a favoured tactic for the Devastators, but the Ospma prided themselves on their resistance to electro-magnetic weaponry.

A *Torrential* exploded as drones swarmed it.

"We're inside the most heavily-armed habitat out here." Kathleen Levy took a deep breath. "What do you think, Doctor?"

"I saw all this back at *Masada*." Anna Boxleitner took a breath and tried to calm her unsteady nerves. *It's not helping.* The flickering displays of the command deck were very distracting.

Levy ignored the crew who were snapping orders and calling out reports. "You seem nervous. Would you care for some chamomile tea?"

"No, thank you."

"As you wish." Levy sipped from her own cup.

"I was at *Masada*."

"And you survived it."

"At least there I was inside a moving ship. Liberty Station can't run away." Anna shook her head.

"True." The light panels dimmed as the crew diverted additional energy to the weapon arrays. "But we have a lot more firepower than any ship. None of the space station's mass or structure has to be dedicated to engines or thrusters either."

"Good point."

"We have an excellent view of the battle." Levy managed to sound unconcerned. She gestured at the displays. "So, as an observer, feel free to offer up whatever comments spring to your mind."

"Shouldn't we be in a shelter?"

"A shelter?"

"Some kind of armoured compartment? Like an old bomb shelter."

"I doubt that would do us much good, Doctor. A sustained barrage from a Devastator's turbolasers would crack pretty much any armoured shelter we could build."

"Oh."

Kathleen sipped on her tea, still pretending to be at ease as she watched the command staff do their jobs. "And bear in mind that should that factory ship reach us, we'll be dead even if we were inside some shelter."

Anan shivered.

A *Deliverance* fired volley after volley from its surge cannon batteries as Devastator drones swarmed around it. Dozens of the tiny craft exploded, but more kept darting in at its flanks. The cruiser finally exploded.

"We just lost the *Bifrost*."

Zane closed his eyes for a moment. *Twelve* Deliverances *lost in this engagement, and two of our missile cruisers. No matter how hard UHW Spacey fights, we keep losing far more ships than the Devastators.*

Boxleitner shook his head. "There's just that one damned ship left!"

Zane nodded. "I know." The carriers had all been destroyed—but that was never much of a challenge. "We just have to deal with that factory ship." Now *that* ship was the challenge.

"And its drones."

"We've weakened it." Wolfgang wiped sweat from his forehead. "Its shielding is intermittent at best."

The once-gleaming hull was blackened in numerous places. The immense factory ship was kilometers long on a side, so the damage was visible to the naked eye.

"Our shots are getting through more often than not." Boxleitner gestured as several missiles struck home in bright explosions.

Kemp grunted. "It just takes so damned long to destroy something that size." The factory ship easily massed more than a habitat.

"The Ospma are launching another attack run."

"Stand by!" Zane watched.

The trio of *Resohexes* accelerated towards the factory ship. Each ship was armed with ten resonance generators and now each fired five forward-facing beams. The fan-shaped beams played across the factory ship's hull.

Zane watched closely. "Wolfgang?" Those resonance generators were nasty devices. They washed a target with opposing electromagnetic fields, causing damage via the resulting shockwaves, as well as overloading circuitry.

"Reading lots of energy fluctuations. It's hurting, Sir."

The *Resohexes* broke off, each firing their five aft-firing beams as they pulled away.

"Its shields are down! Detecting internal explosions."

"Good." Zane smiled. "All ships, fire!"

The Devastator was definitely damaged and its defenses failed further as the remaining UHW Spacey fleet accelerated into range and pounded it with every weapon they could bring to bear.

"Reading an increase in fleet communications!"

Kathleen Levy stared at the main display. The visuals from the battle had been mesmerizing, but it looked like the battle was winding down.

"I think that's the *Hellstorm*." Anna was focusing on one *Endor*-class warship. "I'm sure that it is."

"All ships are firing," the station commander informed them. "Reading wildly fluctuating energy spikes from the target."

"Is that a good sign?"

"Oh yes, Doctor. It's a damn good sign."

Kathleen Levy watched calmly. "I think we're going to win this one."

"I was never worried." Anna Boxleitner nodded, finally matching Levy's false serenity. "My husband is out there."

* * *

"We are greatly reduced in strength and power." Anton Trudeau kept his voice as steady as he could manage while he addressed Parliament. "The United Human Worlds are down to less than ten viable colonies, most of them located within this star system.

"Defending our territory and that of our allies has seen the Seven Fleets whittled away almost to nothing.

"Yet the United Human Worlds still stand. UHW Spacey readies itself for the final battles of this long war."

Parliament was silent.

"Are the rest of the colonies and our Fleets destroyed? Or have they simply gone silent?"

Trudeau looked at Miyaki Hidoshi.

Clark was looking both smug and furious.

"Several more United Human Worlds systems have gone silent," Ashvim Singh spoke up. His Spacey uniform was immaculate, with every single medal that he wore polished. "Before communications were lost, there was no reports of invasions or sightings of enemy ships. We don't know what has happened to them."

"If they were attacked by another race, the United Human Worlds must know! UHW Spacey must send scouts to reestablish communications."

Singh rolled his eyes while the delegate continued to talk.

"Is it true that the Wolf Shipyards were attacked?"

"Member Hidoshi, a small Devastator force is known to have raided the Wolf System. They were all destroyed without inflicting more than minor damage. You all have our assurances that Admiral Sabrina Webber promises to have the Yards fully operational shortly."

"What about Admiral Leftcourt? Where is Seventh Fleet?"

"Dwayne Leftcourt is currently incommunicado. Seventh Fleet is spread throughout Ospma territory, patrolling and fighting within the Baronies. It will take some time for it to reassemble and reach Earth."

"Assuming that the Ospma actually deliver those recall orders...I don't trust all these recent communication disruptions and breakdowns." Clark did not mask the contempt in his voice.

"Shouldn't we have a superior form of communication by now?"

"How can we wage a war when we lack a proper chain-of-command?"

Singh was starting to look annoyed by all the questioning.

Trudeau hastily retook the podium. "I cannot deny that these are dark times. We can only persevere and ready ourselves to fight for the safety of Earth."

"What about the rumour of—"

"Let me dispel the rumours." Singh retook the podium. "We have a massive Devastator fleet heading right towards Earth." He paused, knowing that the shocked outbursts would be louder than he could talk. "At their current speed and course, they will reach firing range of the defensive grid in ten hours." Ashvim Singh looked across the Parliament chamber and his voice was cold, cutting the delegates off in mid-protest. "This could prove to be the decisive battle of the War."

Trudeau winced. *Not could...it* will *be.*

"Can we win this battle?" Luis Santiago demanded.

"Of course we can win." Singh spoke up so that his voice echoed through the room. "The combined might of UHW Spacey is gathering together in orbit even as we speak."

"We are drawing a line," Trudeau said. "One last battle against the night. There is no retreat possible for us, because this is the birth world of the Human Race. I pledge to you that we will fight to the bitter end. No surrender, no retreat."

The room burst into applause.

"No surrender, no retreat!"

Anton Trudeau stepped into the corridor. "That did not go well."

"It never does," Singh agreed as he walked along at a steady pace. "The civilians are not ready to accept the coming war. They need to be guided."

"At least Parliament is behind us."

"Do they have any choice?"

Trudeau chose to ignore the armed troopers in the corridor as they fell into step behind them. "Cynthia," he turned to his chief aide, "I need a shuttle prepped for immediate launch."

The somberly dressed woman nodded. "Of course. For what destination, Prime Minister?"

"I am going into orbit to see our allies."

"The Ospma?" Singh asked after the aide had hurried off.

Trudeau nodded. "Gorpshan is not responding to most of our signals."

"I know. The Ospma are only answering minimally in response to military commands and requests. They are proving to be more reluctant than usual."

"That is not a good thing, is it?"

Singh snorted loudly. "The single greatest battle in history is almost upon us and our main allies—a full *tenth* of our defensive warship strength—has gone silent. I won't stand for it."

"And our other allies?"

"I cannot count on having any other ships than what are currently here." Singh grimaced. "The travel times alone are against us. And too many colonies have vanished...either Devastators or other races. The Spacey is overwhelmed."

"We can't let the civilians hear that."

"Romano has begun deploying her troopers in public places. They will maintain order."

Trudeau looked at him. "At the point of a gun?"

"If necessary. Panic and riot will only cripple us further." Singh paused for a moment. "Have you consulted with Admiral Arden recently?"

Trudeau shook his head. "He has also gone silent."

"I blame his new ally...this Las'li-drac." Singh shook his head, almost spitting out the name. "Another alien power is trying to meddle with the United Human Worlds."

"So far the Raptchi have proven to be helpful," the Prime Minister argued. "They did assist in defeating a Devastator attack."

"And they have since vanished on some unspecified patrols of *our* home star system! They could be amassing strategic data for an invasion!"

"Admiral, if they invade now, they will have the Devastator to fight with. I do not believe Arden would be taken in."

"You assume a great deal, Prime Minister."

"I met this WarMaster briefly. She seemed like an honourable being."

"Alien cultures are not always what they seem."

"True enough, but we can hardly afford to cast off offers from potential allies. This war is draining us. We need to survive it."

"As you say." Singh did not sound convinced of that.

Chapter Twenty-One

"I have some new status reports for you, WarMaster."

"The solar flare activity, Des'ran?" Las'li-drac accepted the hand-held comp-pad and skimmed its display screen. After a few moments, she handed it back to her aide. "I am more interested in enemy fleet distribution. There are far too many Silencer vessels loose in this system and too little information on their deployments."

"They remain a highly mobile enemy," Dale Arden commented as he joined her. "Far too often our scouts encounter them but are destroyed shortly after."

"Your *Endor*-class vessels do leave something to be desired in terms of sensor ability."

"In battles, we often rely on *Scout Wheels* for support and reconnaissance data."

Las'li-drac shook her head at the thought. "That reliance is simply asking for an intelligence failure."

"We've had a few...but the Ospma certainly can't set us up to deliberately fail. I mean, that would jeopardize their own survival in this war."

"So one would assume." She paused a moment. "You have a comment to offer us, Des'ran?"

The other Raptchi nodded. "The Ospma Baronies are located in a region with a high concentration of black holes and other spatial distortions and anomalies. Perhaps their own territory offers them some protection against the Silencers."

Arden frowned. "Admiral Leftcourt has sent back reports about battles with Silencer factory ships in the Baronies."

"Has he personally seen such battles?"

Arden did not reply.

"Any such reported battle could have been staged."

Las'li-drac looked at her aide. "You think they would risk trickery?"

Des'ran grimaced. "They are *Ospma*."

"Faking a battle seems out of character for them." Arden shook his head. "I have traveled to the Comac system and there was definitely a battle fought there. The Seventh Fleet took part in it."

"Tro'han, send word to the Imperium. I want to see some firm and hard proof about Silencer attacks in the Baronies proper."

"As you command, WarMaster." The other Raptchi paused. "And what of the solar readings?"

"What solar readings?"

"We are detecting higher solar emission activity than what is considered normal for your star," Des'ran told the confused-looking Human. "Solar flare activity seems to be increasing."

"I'm having the readings transmitted back to the Science Council for further analysis."

"Good thinking. Solar flares could disrupt our sensors during a battle."

"We should be able to compensate, though hopefully it will affect our enemies even more so. Our sensor systems are hardened more than the Ospma versions. You should alert your fellow Humans though."

"I'll do that." Dale Arden made a note on his own comp-pad. "Odd that the Ospma science ships didn't report this earlier."

Las'li-drac turned towards him with a startled expression on her face. "Science ships? What science ships?"

"Ospma ones. There's been a trio of them studying Sol for a few months now. No, it's closer to a whole year now that I think about it. No wonder that I forgot about them. They've been quiet all this time."

Las'li-drac frowned.

Another Raptchi officer approached them. "WarMaster, we have an incoming signal from the UHW Spacey admiralty. Priority one for Admiral Arden."

Arden accepted the data-crystal and placed it into his reader. "Damn."

"What?"

"A Silencer flotilla has attacked *Leonidas* Station."

Las'li-drac's head whipped around. Her eyes were wide in shock. "What? Your last transit station."

Arden nodded, skimming through the report. "They've heavily damaged it, before being completely destroyed. UHW Spacey isn't certain it can open a wormhole. At least not until it's been repaired."

"And with the current system-wide battles?"

"There's no way we can divert ships to conduct repairs."

"The war grows ever more interesting." A weak smile appeared on her face. "We certainly won't be bored anytime soon."

"No, we won't be, WarMaster."

Las'li-drac turned towards another of her officers and raised her voice. "What is our weapon status, Tro'ha-noa?"

"All systems charged and ready."

"Excellent."

"Are you expecting a battle?"

"I always expect a battle...and I am seldom disappointed."

* * *

Collin Zane frowned. "I still don't approve of this."

"Nor do I," Felix Boxleitner added as technicians hurried past him to service the newly arrived shuttle.

Kathleen Levy stared back at Zane and Boxleitner with a stern expression. "Parliament requested that observers be placed among the Fleets. You saw the orders."

"Tell me that you didn't pull any strings," Zane accused. "Getting yourself assigned to the *Hellstorm*. Just seems a little...preferential?"

"I was as surprised by the transfer orders as you were." Levy had her hair pulled into a tightly braided style due to the zero gravity environment and she had replaced her usual jacket and skirt with a military-styled jumpsuit. "Believe me, I was much happier stationed on Liberty."

"Yeah, you've never liked zero-gee."

"No, it's not just that. Liberty had a lot more firepower available."

Zane snorted. "And a hell of a lot less maneuverability." He paused though, for a moment. "You saw that for yourself when the Devastators attacked."

"We fought them off."

"With heavy losses."

"The zero gee doesn't bother me." Anna had kept silent until that moment. She had been watching the technicians working on the shuttle.

Felix Boxleitner glared at her. "You just came back to me alive and safe, Anna...and now you are going back out into danger. You could get killed out here."

She shook her head. "So could you, Felix."

"It's not safe for you here. This is a warship."

"I was no safer on a science vessel was I?"

"But if you had gotten through the worm—"

"But I didn't. I'm here now though."

The commander sighed and rolled his eyes.

Katheleen smiled at them. "We are both here now and neither of us is leaving." She turned her head. "So you might as well make the best of it, Captain."

Zane grimaced. "She's right, Felix. They're both right."

Anna placed her hand on her husband's arm. "At least this way we'll both be together."

I just hope we don't end up dying together, Zane thought.

* * *

"I am still not satisfied with your report, Miss Winters."

The blonde woman brushed hair out of her eyes. "I submitted a full report to the Bureau upon my return from the Ospma home world, Admiral Singh."

"That report was incomplete."

"It was not!"

Anton Trudeau cleared his throat. "That will do."

"She was supposed to scan the aliens. She should have learned something from their thoughts."

Admiral Lee Hwan Kim coughed into his hand. "She had some mental contact with this Las'li-drac. We need to know more. Did you feel any hint of deception from her?"

"There was deception from everyone," Tabitha Winters replied in a cold tone of voice. "They are *alien*," she explained. "I couldn't read their thoughts clearly."

"But you did sense something?"

"A bit...but it's cold and...well, alien."

"We had this discussion before," Trudeau pointed out.

"And now this Las'li-drac has appeared in the heart of the United Human Worlds and has suborned one of the Joint Chiefs." Lee Hwan Kim shook his head. "This a grave matter. There is a considerable risk of treason."

"I doubt that."

Admiral Ashvim Singh turned towards the speaker with a cruel smile on his face. "Do you, Mrs Trudeau?"

"Of course." Isabelle nodded at him, her expression firm with conviction. "Dale is more loyal to the United Human Worlds than you are."

Singh's face darkened.

Anton Trudeau cleared his throat again. "Working at cross-purposes will not do us any good. We need clear heads if we plan to find a solution to this crisis."

"Yes, Prime Minister."

"We should take a moment to pause and reflect. Bernard, drinks for everyone."

The aide nodded and hurried to the wet-bar.

"If you should think of anything else to add, Miss Winters, you know how to contact us."

She nodded. "Of course."

"Cynthia, see her out."

"Of course." Cynthia Randal stood up gracefully. "This way."

Trudeau turned back to Kim as the door closed behind them. "What word from out-system?"

"Nothing has transited in recently. The rest of the United Human Worlds might as well not even exist for all the data we currently have." Kim did not bother to mask the annoyance in his voice. "Repairs to *Leonidas* have begun, but it will still be at least a week before we can even think about opening a wormhole."

"I have dispatched a sizable force of warships to defend *Leonidas*." Singh paused. "The technicians cannot complain about a lack of protection."

"I've not heard any such complaints." Trudeau accepted his drink. "Thank you, Bernard."

The man nodded silently.

"The Ospma have two *Scout Wheels* present which you might be able to requisition for transiting out ships."

"Unlikely, Kim. The Ospma are loathe to part with them."

"They maintain a monoply on interstellar transit." Singh cursed. "That must change!"

"Wormhole technology is extremely complicated and dangerous to install on something as small as a ship."

"That's crap and you know it, Kim!"

Isabelle grimaced at the outburst.

"Even I know how foolish that is!" Jennifer Romano argued. "The Ospma do it with their *Warspheres* and *Scout Wheels*. The Goolatch do it with their larger ships. Apparently so do these damned Raptchi. From all appearances, we are being kept on a leash."

"The handful of ships which do have worm-engines are exceedingly underarmed and underpowered," Singh pointed out. "It would be suicidal to equip entire fleets with them. Assuming that we could afford to build that many engines."

"Yet if we had more such equipped ships, then we could move civilian traffic, and military convoys, more easily."

"We could ask Admiral Arden to make use of his relationship with Las'li-drac. Perhaps they have a solution superior to what the Ospma use."

"No."

"Why not, Singh?"

"The Ospma are a known quality...these Raptchi are not."

Isabelle was staring through the window into the Green Well.

There was a knock at the door.

"Enter!" Trudeau watched a man enter. He was wearing a dark blue uniform with insignia and rank pins. "Prime Minister." He nodded. "Admiral Singh." He offered a salute.

"Yes?" Trudeau had no idea who the man was. *He's got insignia for the Psionic Oversight Bureau.* "Miss Winters has already departed."

"I'm not here for her. Nathan Fisk."

"What do you want, Lieutenant Fisk?"

Fisk turned towards Singh. "I am aware that you did not wish to be disturbed, Admiral, but we have just a report from the *Wandering Fire.* I think it's rather important."

"Oh?" Trudeau turned away from talking softly to his wife. "What did they say?"

"We have a visual feed." Fisk inserted a data-crystal into the reader on the desk.

A painting on the wall flickered, then darkened, and abruptly lit up with a visual of Devastator factory ships.

"My God!" Isabelle grabbed her husband's arm.

"This was a live transmission," Fisk informed.

Scores of the blocky factory ships were advancing across space, with hundreds of carriers to accompany them.

"Where is this from?" Romano demanded.

"Far side of Sol...roughly Mars orbit."

The image flared and went dark.

"We estimate forty factory ships, five hundred carriers, and God know how many combat drones." Fisk gestured to the now-dark display. "Contact with *Wandering Fire* was lost. We can't raise her."

Trudeau winced.

"What course are those ships on?"

"Direct vector for Earth." Fisk's lips twitched into a weak smile. "You can see why I thought the signal might be important."

"It's the final battle."

"I should call a session of Parliament."

"I would not bother." Singh shook his head. "It will just be a waste of time to listen to them bicker."

"Admiral!"

"Do you want to call a news conference? Tell the world that every Devastator in the galaxy is bearing down on Earth?" Singh laughed bitterly. "Do that and you *will* have riots in the streets! Romano's ground forces will have something to do...trying to keep the civilians from killing each other."

"We are democracy."

"Then start a panic." Singh rose to his feet. "I will be gathering UHW Spacey for the battle." He nodded at Kim. "Come along, Fisk. We have recall signals to send out."

* * *

Scores of the blocky factory ships were advancing across space. Hundreds of carriers covered their flanks and swarms of drones buzzed around them.

"So many ships." Arden could barely believe his eyes as he studied the visual display. "So bloody many ships."

"I have never seen so many gathered in one place before." Las'li-drac was smiling as she prowled along her flag bridge. "This will be a battle worthy of the most ancient and epic legends!" she exclaimed. "History will long remember this day!"

The UHW Spacey Admiral looked at her. "Hopefully we will be alive to remember it with them."

"I have no fear of that." She waved a hand. "Additional vessels have arrived from the Imperium to support my operations here. The Silencers cannot stand up to repeated assaults from my battle *pentacons*."

"WarMaster." Des'ran approached them. "We have a communication intercept from Earth. The Prime Minister has issued emergency orders for all UHW Spacey vessels to rendez-vous in Earth orbit."

"A line in the sand," Arden commented softly.

"The final battle is almost upon us." The WarMaster chuckled and rubbed her hands together. "It will be a glorious fight."

"Will we arrive in time?"

"Of course." Las'li-drac gestured. "Are the fleet's worm-engines are charged?"

"Yes, WarMaster."

Las'li-drac turned. "What other ships do you still have, Admiral?"

"Other ships?" He frowned.

"The recall has been issued but it will take time for your ships to travel here. You must have other task forces still scattered throughout this system."

"Not many, Las'li-drac. UHW Spacey has pretty much already gathered itself into Earth orbit."

"A pity. I was willing to transit out and gather them up...under your command of course."

Arden shook his head grimly. "There's nothing left to gather."

Chapter Twenty-Two

"The final battle is about to begin."

Collin Zane stared at the bridge displays. "Then let's make it a good one, Commander."

"We will, Sir." Felix Boxleitner nodded.

"All missile bays loaded and standing by."

"Engines are primed."

Zane took a deep breath. "Then we now await the final order from Fleet Command."

Ashvim Singh gripped the railing of the balcony more tightly. From his vantage, he could see all of the officers and technicians who worked at the multi-level room's computer stations and plotting tanks. *So many young people working so hard to defend their homeworld.* How could anyone not feel pride at this sight?

"Are you certain you do not wish to observe the battle from the surface?"

Singh shook his head. "No, General Franklin. I am the supreme commander of what remains of UHW Spacey," he replied. "I will live or die with my troops."

"As you wish, Admiral." Richard Franklin nodded his understanding, and his own approval, of that.

"There still aren't enough of them for you, are there?"

"No."

Singh raised his voice. "What's the status of the OWPs?"

"All elements of the defence grid are reporting their readiness for battle. Missile racks are fully stocked and their reactors are fully charged. Targeting systems are programmed and ready to engage."

Franklin had sent technical crews to check over each one in the last few weeks. "The minefields have been replenished as well."

"Ship status?"

"All squadrons have been assigned to a starting position, and every squadron knows where to proceed as the battle lines shift. The Ospma are integrated with the rest of the Fleets."

Singh grimaced. "And what of Arden's new friends?"

"The Raptchi were last seen gathering near the moon, with a handful of the lunar garrison joining them. Armstrong City has stopped transmitting."

"Could Arden be trying to build of type of fall-back position?"

"Possibly." Franklin did not sound convinced of that.

Singh sipped from a glass of water, then handed it to an aide.

"Factory ships are continuing to approach at a steady pace," Franklin pointed out. Observed tactics in numerous battles had shown that factory ships simply kept coming until they were destroyed. "This is going to be one hell of a battle."

"The most important in Human history."

Franklin said nothing.

"I know that we have had our differences in the past," Singh said slowly. "We have clashed over tactics and over strategy."

Franklin looked surprised, but then he nodded. "Yes, we have."

"It was never personal, you do know that?"

"Yes, I suppose I did." Franklin took a breath. "It's been a pleasure serving with you, Admiral."

"And with you, General. Freedom Station is yours to command. I have no intention of interfering with its defence."

"You have to command the larger battle."

"Exactly. There are so few command-level officers left." The rest of the Joint Chiefs were scattered or dead by now. *Romano thinks she can hold out on the surface...once a factory ship enters orbit, then it's all over down there.*

"Yes, I understand." Franklin adjusted his headset and looked at Singh. "Prime Minister Trudeau has taken a shuttle over to the Ospma flagship."

"Why?"

"I have no idea."

Singh frowned. "I thought he was planning to join us here on the command deck. That was why he shuttled up with me...or so he said." *Does he plan to try and escape from the fall of Earth on an Ospma ship?* He could not believe that. *Trudeau would never leave his wife behind to die.*

"The Devastators are continuing to advance."

Singh raised his voice. "I want to transmit a message to all ships."

"Standing by."

He took a deep breath. "This is Admiral Singh to all commands. You all know exactly what is at stake here—we have nowhere left to retreat. UHW Spacey must hold the line. The survival of Humanity depends on it." He closed his eyes. "Good luck to us all."

Franklin turned to his staff.

"They're launching drones."

"Surge cannons charged and ready to fire."

"Release the advance wave," Singh ordered. "Activate all ECM."

"ECM jamming on-line."

"We have drones accelerating."

"Hopefully the minefields will be able to slow them." Franklin did not sound very hopeful.

An *Endor*-class frigate broke formation, advancing towards the lead wave of carriers along with a dozen *Deliverances*. Their surge cannons began firing as drones closed with them.

Explosions began to erupt on the *Hellstorm's* main display.

"The minefields are getting some of them," Wolfgang reported.

"Not enough though." Collin Zane shook his head. "The drones are too fast."

"At least those twin ion engines give us a good targeting lock."

"Kemp, have your gunners stand by. Things are going to get messy."

General Franklin stood on the command deck watching his staff. "Fire all batteries as soon as you have range."

"Drones entering weapons range."

"Shunting power to surge cannons! Tracking targets."

"Targets acquired. Firing now!"

The lights dimmed as the weapon batteries drew more power from the station's reactors.

"Enemy drones firing!"

"I hope you have sealed off the bulkheads." Singh had been silent for some time, but now he spoke up. As an experienced spacer, he could feel the vibrations of distant impacts. His eyes sought out the station status display and took note of flashing icons. *No serious hits as yet.*

"It will take more than a few drones to knock *Freedom* out of the fight." General Franklin grinned, his teeth startling bright in the dimly-lit command deck. "Their little raid last month has given the gunners plenty of practice picking them off."

"Aided by your infamous snap drills?"

"Heard about them did you?" Franklin's grin grew wider. "I think they proved themselves ready for a fight."

"Carriers are entering OWP range."

"Clear the OWPs to begin firing. I want those ships destroyed before they can launch more drones."

The heavy OWPs opened fire and laser beams and missiles lashed at the carriers.

Drones dove towards the weapon satellites, and surge cannons swatted them from the sky.

Singh licked his lips and watched the displays.

A *Witch of Endor* was swarmed by drones and blew apart.

Surge cannon bolts from a *Deliverance* cruiser raked a carrier.

An Ospma *Scout Wheel* raked a factory ship with its surge cannon, following with a barrage from its electro-magnetic pulsars.

Two *Torrential* missile cruisers began salvoing their missiles into the hull of the massive factory ship as fast as they could reload their launchers.

"Multiple explosions detected...the factory ship is hurt." But it was a large target and it would take time for even nuclear warheads to fully cripple it. "Energy spike...we've lost the *Duan Gung's* transponder!"

Zane winced. *Torrential* missile cruisers were extremely vulnerable to enemy fire and one good hit to any magazine was crippling.

"We're holding them, right?"

"For now." Felix Boxleitner shook his head. "But it's costing us."

"This could be a Phyrric victory." Zane shook his own head.

"Better a victory than defeat," Levy commented. "Given the alternative for us." Anna Boxleitner and Kathleen Levy had no place on the bridge, but Zane had failed to order them below decks before the battle began.

"The Ospma are fighting this time. That give us a chance, right?"

"A slim one, Doctor Boxleitner." Zane was under no illusions about UHW Spacey's chances in this war. *We hold or we die...there will be no second chances.* "Wolfgang, keep our jammers going."

"Aye, Captain."

Kemp snapped orders to his gunners.

"I've not heard reports of any more Devastators arriving." Kathleen spoke up. "Maybe they've run out of reinforcements."

"They'll just build more." Boxleitner tapped a control on his console. "They're like locusts...spreading and multiplying as they go."

"Then we just can't let them go any further." Zane cleared his throat. "That factory ship has reached Strike Point. Jankowski, take us forward. Maximum thrust."

"A dozen firefights." Las'li-drac studied a display. "Glorious isn't it?"

"It would be more glorious if those firefights didn't meant the deaths of hundreds of people."

"Of course, I'm sorry." The Raptchi WarMaster turned. "Your people are putting up a valiant defence. They shattered the first wave of drones." Hundreds of the deadly craft were just floating debris now.

"But it won't be enough." Arden pointed to the screen. "Here come the big boys."

The carriers swept forward, spilling more drones from their hangers.

"They've kept substantial reserves." Las'li-drac chuckled. "A good plan...the Silencer drones were not exposed to any of your long-range fire during their approach, and they managed to weaken your defences."

"Slightly." Earth was strongly fortified after all. "The OWPs are firing now...and they're scoring hits." Carriers were easy targets and lasers and missiles were striking hard. "We're killing a lot before they can launch."

"It won't be enough."

"They're working to wear us down before the kill." Arden smiled as one carrier was struck by multiple mines and blew apart.

"We'll have to disappoint them then."

The *Hellstorm* fired its surge cannon batteries, accompanied by fire from three other *Deliverances* and missiles from two *Torrential* cruisers.

"Multiple hits on target," Wolfgang reported. "It looks like we've disabled their thrusters."

"Continue firing. Engine damage is good, but destroying them entirely would be better."

"Captain, the Devastators are launching a major push!"

Zane looked at the display. "Damn it!" Three factory ships were moving forward, flanked by a dozen carriers. "Stand by to engage."

"But we haven't destroyed the first one yet."

"Those ones will be on top of us before we can finish it off, Kemp. Call for reinforcements."

"I'm not sure there are any."

"Alert Freedom Station of this!" Boxleitner snapped. "We need reinforcements."

Zane bit his lip. UHW Spacey was being scattered, too few ships to defend against too many targets. "It's not much of a line," he grumbled.

"Devastator ships are pushing through sector four mark two. The main defense line is crumbling."

Franklin snapped a curse.

Singh cursed softly. "We don't have anything in position to arrive in time." The reserves for that area had already been committed to another skirmish. "We'll have to rely on mines and OWPs."

"It won't be enough," Franklin told him.

"The inner defense grid will have to hold them off."

"Admiral, we have an energy disruption in that sector!"

"What?"

"Energy spike!"

"Brace for weapon impacts!" Zane ordered.

"It's not weaponry!" Wolfgang said. "Wormhole opening!"

"Get me a visual!"

There was ripple and a massive wormhole swirled open.

"I've seen this before!" Collin Zane failed to keep a smile from his face as the opening vortex clipped two separate factory ships and the massive vessels were torn apart by fiery explosions which also served to destroy several carriers and countless drones.

"Ships leaving the vortex...reading Raptchi transponder beacons!"

"WarMaster Las'li-drac." Zane smiled in pure relief. "Open a comm-channel."

"I do enjoying making a lasting impression." Las'li-drac waved her hand rather imperiously. "Gunners, I see no shortage of targets for you."

"Your transit precision is impressive, WarMaster."

"Decades of practice, Admiral Arden," she replied. "As a weapon, it is most devastating to any foe. There is no method of surviving it...ship or station, the energy rips matter apart at a molecular level. Or so I believe. None of our close-range research probes last long enough to provide us with meaningful data."

"Enemy drones closing."

"Target the carrier, Tro'ha-noa."

"Firing missile racks."

"Pulsar barrage to cover them." She glanced towards Arden. "Hopefully the pulsars will distract the drones."

"Missiles are the only weapons that seem to do any serious damage to their larger ships."

"Until we can wear down their shields at any rate."

Arden watched the display as the Raptchi squadron shattered a carrier and swarmed a factory ship. "I have always found it strange that the Silencers have never adapted their shield technology to block projectiles."

"I do not believe the Silencers are programmed to think. They use what weaponry they were designed with and nothing more."

"Energy spike from Target-Beta."

The dreadnaught shuddered.

Arden could hear the bulkheads groaning as the ship flexed under the stress of multiple impacts. *No alert klaxons though.*

"Ray shields holding."

"Return fire," Las'li-drac ordered calmly.

"Bearing on factory ship. Transponder reads...*Silencer-Two-Twelve*."

"Fire primary weapon."

Arden opened his mouth to ask what the primary weapon was when the lights dimmed and the deck plates lurched under his feet. "Are we hit?"

Las'li-drac smiled calmly. "No, just firing the main gun."

A bright flash lit the hull of the factory ship as hull armour shattered and erupted into space.

Arden stared. "What the hell was that?" Secondary explosions were erupting from points on the hull.

"A round from our mass driver." Las'li-drac typed a command and studied the sensor readings. "Just as effective against Silencers as it is against planets."

Arden blinked.

* * *

"So many ships." Anton Trudeau finally had to shake his head in simple disbelief. *So many ships.* He was sitting on the cold floor—this particular *Warsphere* was built to Ospma-scale and none of the rooms or corridors were tall enough to allow a Human to do more than crouch. *It is most undignified for me to have to crawl through the corridors to see Gorpshan,* he thought. *And this ship is designed better than most to accommodate visitors.* The Ospma seldom left their ships after all. He cleared his throat, trying not to notice the humidity in the air. "There are a lot of enemy ships."

"Yes." Gorpshan was seated in the centre of the room, surrounded by displays and control systems. He reached out tentacle-arms to grasp at wires.

It's all so silent. Trudeau saw no other crewmembers, nor did he hear any chatter echoing through bridge speakers. *Aside from machinery, this ship is completely silent. It's not like any UHW Spacey ship I've been on.* He was technically in the corridor—there was simply not enough room for him to enter the bridge, such as it was. "There must be thousands of them." He stared at the displays that ringed the walls of the bridge. *So many ships.* That thought was quickly followed by another. *I'm getting dizzy trying to watch all these screens.* "I've never seen so many factory ships in one place before."

"You have lured many here."

Trudeau frowned. "Lured?"

"With each battle won, you draw more of the enemy towards you. Prove yourself more threat. This system is now a very high priority for them."

"But we can defend it...right?"

"Each new wave comes in greater strength." Gorpshan reached for another wire and coiled one of his tentacles around it. "The final gambit can now be played."

"What gambit?" Trudeau blinked repeatedly. Firefights were already erupting on the displays as the inner defensive perimeter became active. *So many dead already...how many more to join them?* "Gorpshan, where are your ships?"

The Ospma said nothing.

"Where are the rest of our allies?"

Gorpshan wrapped a tentacle-arm around a comm-line as it vibrated.

"We can't hold without support. Gorpshan!"

"The bait has proven tasty." The *Warsphere* lurched as it finally powered up its engines and broke orbit. "We go now."

"Go?" Trudeau gestured helplessly towards the battle.

A warm mauve colour washed over the Ospma's mottled skin. "The final gambit is played...the victory is ours."

"Gorpshan, what are you saying?"

* * *

"Devastator factory ship is breaking through sector five-one."

"Hit it with everything in the area!" Singh ordered loudly.

That portion of the defense grid was still intact and the OWPs began firing. A few mines exploded against the factory ship's hull as well.

"Admiral, we're detecting increased solar flare activity."

"Ignore it. I don't have time for trivialities right now."

Freedom Station rocked.

"Carrier ship in range, launching additional drones."

"Fire surge cannons on those drones!" General Franklin ordered. "Ready all missile racks to fire. Take down that carrier."

"Ready to fire."

One display showed a *Deliverance* being swarmed by drones.

"*Ti Ts'ang* reporting total power loss. Their reactor is off-line."

"First Fleet is taking a pounding."

"I can see that."

"*Yu Huang* moving to cover."

"Can we get in closer? Give them support fire?"

"Not at this time, Admiral."

Franklin moved closer to Singh. "I'm not sure how long we can sustain this level of combat."

"We'll sustain it for as long as we have too," Singh snarled. "We don't have any other choice."

"Las'li-drac, how long can you keep this up?"

"For as long your own people can." The WarMaster bared her teeth in a feral smile. "I will not surrender this world to my enemies," she vowed. "The Silencers must be destroyed at whatever cost we must pay."

"We've destroyed a hell of lot of them." UHW Spacey and its allies had paid a heavy price in doing so though. "Even the Silencers have to break at some point."

"We have never seen a factory ship break off its attack, Admiral." She paused. "Still, there is always a first time."

Arden nodded.

"WarMaster, the Ospma fleet is breaking off their attacks."

"What?" She turned. "Confirm that!"

A pair of satellites fired their missile racks and a carrier exploded.

"It's confirmed. The Ospma are pulling back...fighting their way free of all engagements."

Arden stared at the displays. "I don't understand."

"So much for them loyally supporting their slaves."

"Las'li-drac, we are not their slaves."

"They're not helping their *allies* out very much then." She gestured at the displays. "They're running away."

"But why?"

"I don't know."

"WarMaster, solar flare activity is increasing."

"Still?"

Arden was more concerned with the course the Ospma ships were following. *Why did they abandon us?* "Hopefully those flares will play havoc with the Devastators."

"It's not going to do our own sensors very much good either."

"A risk we have to take."

Fire from several OWPs converged on a factory ship. Its shielding failed and explosions lit its hull.

Wolfgang cursed. "A second factory ship is moving up...it's attempting to tractor in the debris."

"To recycle it into more weaponry."

"Why aren't the OWPs targeting the second ship?" Kathleen Levy asked softly.

"A wave of drones have engaged them," Felix Boxleitner told her. "The satellites are being destroyed."

"The Devastators are weakening us enough to break through to reach Earth."

"Call up some support!" Levy gasped. "We need reinforcements."

"Transmitting now."

Zane shook his head. "They'll wear us down and just keep coming."

Anna nodded. "As long as one factory ship is operational, they can replicate themselves and rebuild their strength."

Zane chuckled. "So we'll just have to destroy all of them," he announced. "No problem, right Felix?"

"I'll have to requisition more nukes then."

"Do that, Commander."

"Divine Wind Squadron-Beta-Three is breaking orbit."

Zane closed his eyes. "Give them some cover fire!" The shuttles were accelerating as quickly as they could.

"Drones closing on intercept vectors."

"Cover fire now, Kemp!"

"Firing all batteries."

The surge cannons fire and drones exploded.

"Shuttles closing."

The factory ship fired its laser batteries and several shuttles exploded in powerful fireballs.

The survivors broke through the defensive barrage and rammed the hull.

"No survivors from the shuttles."

Las'li-drac turned to look at Arden. "You look surprised."

"That was one of Singh's strategies," he muttered. "Divine Wind, he called it." He shook his head. "I never thought he would actually use it."

"It appears to be successful." The factory ship was crippled; most of its hull was heavily cratered and its energy grid was off-line.

"Though far too costly."

"A few shuttles in exchange for a factory ship? A bargain at twice the price I dare say."

Arden's eyes widened.

"A most ruthless tactic," Las'li-drac continued. "I did not think your race had it in you to be martyrs."

"Earth is our home world. There are billions of us down there. We can't let them die."

"No...." She tapped her fingers against the arm of her chair.

"WarMaster, I'm detecting serious disturbances in the corona."

"This is hardly the time for a science report!" she snapped at him. "We have the biggest battle in history raging out there. There must still be a hundred factory ships coming this way now, and with thousands of escorts."

"But the sun...if these readings are right, the sun is becoming unstable."

"*Unstable*?" Arden repeated.

"Yes."

"The Ospma!"

Arden looked at Las'li-drac after her outburst. "What about them?"

She had bared her teeth in a furious snarl. "They're masters of manipulating quantum singularities...what would happen if they detonated one of those singularities inside the sun?"

Arden frowned. "I have no idea." He shrugged helplessly.

Las'li-drac shook her head. "It could result in a serious disruption to the normal solar processes...and cause these massive flares. Or worse."

"Worse?"

"A nova."

Arden shook his head in disbelief. "No way. I don't believe they would even attempt such a thing!"

"They could be trying to trigger a nova." Las'li-drac sounded intrigued, even fascinated by the idea. "Their ultimate Silencer-destroying weapon."

"No," Arden muttered.

"Destroy the machine fleet in one blow...and eliminate all of us in the process."

All eyes turned towards the sun.

"Solar activity is increasing exponentially. Approaching critical levels."

"Deactivate all weapons!" Las'li-drac bellowed and Arden cringed at the ferocity in her voice. "Charge the worm-engine and open a vortex. Copy that to all ships...priority gold!"

"As you command, WarMaster."

Arden licked his lips as the feeling of the bridge changed from eagerness to fear. "Can you open a wormhole this close to Earth?"

"We are certainly going to try."

Arden closed his eyes.

"I've seen the records from Raptarachi when it's star went nova...I have no desire to be anywhere in the area when Sol follows suit." The Raptchi officer shook her head, pride mingling with horror in her voice. "We've won a victory here...now we just have to live long enough to enjoy it."

"But Earth...."

"Cannot be saved."

Arden's mouth hung open.

"Signal all Human ships to form up around us as we withdraw. Our ships will hold the wormholes open for as long as we possibly can."

Arden was staring through the armoured viewport as the battle continued to rage. "All those people down there."

"Casualties of war." She shrugged, clearly uncertain of what else she could say. "Avenge them later...the Ospma will pay." She placed her hand on his shoulder. "We will finally be able to live without the fear of the Silencers."

"But that's my home world."

"We will rebuild," she told him, "and then we will seek our revenge."

Discover other titles by Matt Kirkby at Smashwords.com:

Connect with Me Online:

Smashwords: http://www.smashwords.com/profile/view/MattKirkby

Facebook: http://facebook.com/MattKirkby

Also by Matt Kirkby

A Novel of Lovecraftian Horror
The Death of Hope

Stories Of Feudal Japan
With Honour Veiled

Standalone
A Wyrm In the Heart
Cthonian Dragons
Forlorn Gambit
Reap What Has Been Sown
The Horror From The Sea
Vector Of Infection

About the Author

Born and raised in small-town Ontario, Matt Kirkby is a romantic dreamer who specializes in writing tales of high fantasy and pulp-style science fiction and space operas. He draws his inspiration from all diverse sources and ideas: Science Fiction, Fantasy, Gothic Horror, Pastoral Nature. He started his writing career submitting fan fiction for numerous Star Wars and TransFormers fanzines, but has since moved on to writing professionally. He published his first novel, A Wyrm In The Heart in 2004. He lives a double life, writing classy sci-fi and fantasy for fun under his own name, and penning gay erotica under the pen name of Frank Sol. When not writing, Matt spends his time helping his partner with his hand-crafted rocking chair business -- www.OffYourRocker.ca -- and trying to maintain some control over his cat. He still thinks that no gift is better than a new book.